# Captain Vampire

# Captain Vampire

by
**Marie Nizet**

translated, annotated and introduced by
**Brian Stableford**

A Black Coat Press Book

**Acknowledgements:** We are indebted to Robert Eighteen-Bisang of Transylvania Press, PO Box 75012, WRPO White Rock, BC Canada V4B 5L3, and to David McDonnell for proofreading the typescript.

Visit our website at www.blackcoatpress.com

# Introduction

Marie Nizet's *Le Capitaine Vampire*, originally published in Paris in 1879 by Auguste Ghio, was lost to sight for more than a century. The Bibliothèque Nationale has no copy, nor has the British Library or the Library of Congress. The book was rediscovered by Radu Florescu, a Rumanian scholar who had made something of a specialty out of researching the historical background of Bram Stoker's *Dracula* (1897) and the Voivode on which the eponymous character was modeled, Vlad Dragul, *alias* the Impaler. One of Florescu's successors, Matei Cazacu, appended a reprint of Nizet's novella to his own compound biography (in French) of the historical and literary figures, *Dracula* (2004), and included a chapter in his commentary speculating about its possible influence on Stoker.

Cazacu's research into Marie Nizet's background revealed that she was born in Brussels on January 18, 1859–which means that she had not long turned 20 when *Le Capitaine Vampire* was published, presumably having written it at 19. Her father, François-Joseph Nizet (1829-1899), was a lawyer whose numerous political pamphlets, of a fervently patriotic stripe, had won him an appointment as the joint curator of the Bibliothèque Royale; while occupying that position, he published various scholarly works in the fields of bibliography and history. Marie's younger brother, Henri (1863-1925), also embarked on a literary career as a journalist and novelist.

Although Henri remained in Brussels to pursue his studies, Marie went to Paris to complete her education, where she cultivated a strong interest in Rumanian culture and folklore. In 1878, she published a volume of poetry entitled *România*; Cazacu observes that many of its inclusions are based on native ballads celebrating the continual wars of independence fought against the Turks of the Ottoman Empire, but that her political commentary takes even greater offence at the treatment of Rumania by the "great powers" whose international conferences strove to settle "the Turkish question" in the 1870s–with the eventual result that Rumania became a pawn of Russian imperial ambitions in the Russo-Turkish war of 1877-78, which forms the historical background of the story told in *Le Capitaine Vampire*.

Marie Nizet never visited Rumania; her knowledge of the country and its predicament was very largely based on information provided by two close friends: Euphrosyna and Virgilia Radulescu, the daughters of the late writer and fervently anti-Russian political agitator Ion Heliade Radulescu (1802-1872). Radulescu was considered to be the foremost 19th-century representative of Rumanian culture; he founded and edited the first Rumanian newspaper and played a leading role in the 1848 "Muntenian revolution," becoming a member of the provisional government set up thereafter. He was well-known in France, and contributed articles to many of the leading French newspapers.

For Marie, under the spell of Euphrosyna and Virgilia, Rumania became part of that Parisian land of dreams called "the Orient," to which many Parisian writers made imaginary pilgrimages, if not actual ones. She seems to have found it very easy to empathize with her friends' patriotism, and their indignation at the Tsar's abuse of his Rumanian allies. The centerpiece of her story–the fulcrum around which everything else is organized–is an account of the storming of the Gravitza redoubt on September 11, 1877, when several regiments of the Rumanian army were ordered by their Russian commander-in-chief to lead a dangerous assault that had a tremendous cost in human lives.

Cazacu, whose only focus of interest is the character of "Captain Vampire" himself, suggests that the inspiration for the novella might have come from one of Ion Heliade Radulescu's poems, *Zburàtoral*, which describes a young girl's sexual awakening in response to the visitation of an incubus. Nizet's novella has a very different theme, though, and the most obvious literary influences manifest in the novella are two of Charles Perrault's didactic fairy tales, known in English as "Cinderella" and "Little Red Riding-Hood."

In studiously echoing these moral tales, Nizet is not attempting to produce an "art fairy tale" of the kind beloved by some Romantic writers, but quite the reverse; she refers to the stories primarily to mock and deny them, calling attention by contrast to the fact that real life is not at all like a fairy tale. Although its plot has supernatural elements, and its antagonist is manifestly demonic, the eponymous monster is part of a more elaborate pattern of symbolism whose purpose is to bring out the horror of actual events. First and foremost, and in its very essence, *Le Capitaine Vampire* is a war story, and a very striking one. In its method and tone alike, it was way ahead of its time, and the principal reason for the book's rapid descent into obscurity might well have been its discomfitingly cynical treatment of the ugliness of warfare–a treatment that must have seemed more than slightly shocking as the composition of a young woman of 19.

We are now so accustomed to reading fiction of the "war is hell" variety, including fiction dealing with contemporary wars, that it is easy to forget how recent a literary product it is. War is surprisingly inconspicuous among the topics of early literature; such battles as are featured in literature before 1800–the siege of Troy in Homer's *Iliad*, the First Crusade in *Gerusalemme Liberata* (1580) by Torquato Tasso and the battle of Agincourt in William Shakespeare's *Henry V* (1600) are among the most famous examples–were invariably distanced by history to the extent of having become legendary. Countless writers active between the era of Geoffrey Chaucer's knight and the American Revolution lived through wars, but almost none offered any substantial account of them; the conventional manner of representing past battles was to present them as arenas of glorious heroism.

Hans von Grimmelshausen was probably the first writer to incorporate the legacy of his own experience– he was press-ganged into the Thirty Years War at the age of 13–into a major literary work, the satirical novel *Simplicissimus* (1669; tr. 1912). However, Grimmelshausen's demolition by mockery of the guiding myths of "aristocratic warfare"–duty, chivalry and heroism–stood virtually alone for more than a century. Similar analyses only began to emerge in numbers when the era of "political warfare" began as the slow spread of democratic responsibility began to engage whole populations–tacitly, at least–in matters of diplomatic propriety. That was the context in which Napoleon Bonaparte became a legend in his own lifetime, but the most notable dramatic account of the battle of Waterloo (1815) was not written until Stendhal produced *La Chartreuse de Parme* (*The Charterhouse of Parma*; 1839) a generation later.

The business and representation of war were irrevocably altered by the Crimean War of 1854-56, which was the first to be extensively reported in the press. The highly critical running commentary provided by the London *Times* mobilized popular opinion so successfully that the public became intoxicated by its newly-discovered right of censure and laid virtual siege to Parliament, while the military complained bitterly that all its secrets were being given away. The combatants in the Crimea included Leo Tolstoy, but he preferred to look back at a more distanced conflict in compiling his massive quasi-sociological study of *War and Peace* (1863-69).

The American Civil War of 1861-65 was reported even more conscientiously than the Crimean War, with the additional luxury of illustrative photography. The reportage of the Crimean and American Civil Wars–especially the latter–provided the imaginative kindling for the genre of contemporary war poetry, the vast majority of the works collected thereafter being written by civilians reacting to the news, but prose fiction featuring their major battles was more belated.

The Franco-Prussian War of 1870-71 made a brutal impact on the many writers who lived in Paris; they had to suffer the siege of the city and the consequent bloody reign of the Commune. Even that experience, however, did not call forth a swift response in the form of substantial works of prose fiction set against the background of the war. The sharp example set by Bismarck's relentlessly efficient army did give prompt birth to a significant subgenre of future war stories, pioneered in Britain by George T. Chesney's ingeniously alarmist *The Battle of Dorking*, but most of the early works comprising that genre were jingoistic celebrations of potential conquest rather than reflections on the potential horrors of future warfare.

In 1879, therefore, the subgenre of contemporary war fiction hardly existed, and the subgenre of contemporary anti-war fiction did not exist at all. There was nothing with which to compare Marie Nizet's *Le Capitaine Vampire* in its own day, and even when the Great War of 1914-18–the first in which press coverage became a heavily-censored vehicle of propaganda–began to generate reactive literary works on a massive scale, very little was produced that used techniques of symbolic exaggeration similar to those that Nizet found convenient.

As a war story therefore, *Le Capitaine Vampire*–which deals with a key event that had taken place less than two years before its publication–may be reckoned to have languished without the remotest parallel for at least half a century. Seen in that light, there is a certain irony in the fact that it has only begun to attract attention again because of its status as a vampire story, and its possible influence on the most famous vampire novel of all. Given that this is the case, however, the issue must be squarely addressed.

The possibility of the novella's possible influence on Bram Stoker cannot be sensibly discussed without extensive reference to its plot, so that sort of speculation is best left to an afterword, where it cannot spoil the reader's enjoyment in advance. It is, however, appropriate to offer a brief consideration here of the earlier history of French vampire fiction, in order to identify the groundwork on which Nizet might have been able to draw in selecting and shaping her key motif.

Cazacu observes that Marie Nizet's text does not employ any of the Rumanian words associated with vampire folklore–he lists *strigoï, vârcolac, moroi* and *nosferatu*–but only the word "vampire" itself. He notes that the word is of Slavic origin, but that is unlikely to be of any significance; by 1879 it had become common-place in French parlance and it is with its French meaning that Nizet concerns herself. Indeed, she makes no reference at all to vampire folklore, although almost everyone else who wrote 19th-century French fiction featuring vampires seems to have had some knowledge of the contents of Dom Augustin Calmet's classic treatise on the subject, first published in 1746, even if that information had been filtered through the popular collection *Infernaliana* (1822; belatedly attributed, perhaps dubiously, to Charles Nodier).

*Infernaliana*'s selective recycling of Calmet's "case studies" includes a substantial chapter on "Vampires de Hongrie," which is presumably responsible for the fact that most 19th-century French vampire novels feature Hungarian vampires rather than Rumanian ones. Nizet shows not the slightest evidence of familiarity with *Infernaliana* or its source, or of having taken any notice of such elements in later texts shaped under its influence.

There were, however, other significant inputs to the development of the French literary mythology of the vampire, of which the most important was John Polidori's novelette *The Vampyre* (1819), which was rapidly translated into French. *The Vampyre* gave rise to several imitative works, including two successful dramatic adaptations, both entitled *Le Vampire* and both produced at the Porte-Saint-Martin theatre, in 1820 (a version adapted by Achille Jouffroy d'Abbans, Jean-Toussaint Merle and Charles Nodier) and 1851 (a version further adapted by Alexandre Dumas and Auguste Maquet).[1]

Although it is highly unlikely that Nizet had seen the play performed, she might well have read the script of Dumas' version in the 1876 edition of his collected plays, just as she might easily have read a translation of Polidori's original. Both texts feature male vampires, as Nizet's does, but this was relatively rare in early 19th-century French literature; the texts she could have found even more easily–including Théophile Gautier's *nouvelle* "*La morte amoureuse*" (1836; tr. as "*Clarimonde*" or "*The Dead Leman*") and two poems from Charles Baudelaire's *Les fleurs du mal* (1857), "*Le vampire*" and "*Les métamorphoses du vampire*," employ the word in a psychosexual context with respect to female temptresses (although Baudelaire's use of the masculine pronoun suggests that it is male lust rather than the female object of desire that he is characterizing as vampiric).

The only other text Nizet is likely to have run across which features a male vampire is Paul Féval's *La ville vampire* (1867 as a serial),[2] whose first book version was issued in 1875 and must still have been available for purchase when she arrived in Paris. Although Féval's novella is a historical comedy parodying the excesses of English Gothic fiction, it does have two features that are found nowhere else prior to 1879 and which are reproduced in *Le Capitaine Vampire*: the vampire's ability to be in two places at once, and an extensive exercise in symbolism that makes vampirism a

[1] (See Notes p. 159.)

12

lurid exaggeration of various sorts of human depredation, including those associated with warfare. The former is trivial, but the latter may be more significant.

The word "vampire" was extensively used in a metaphorical sense before 1879. Baudelaire's use of it as a symbol of the male response to female sexuality reflected a trend that eventually gave rise to the American use of the term "vamp" as a description of predatory women–especially those featured in the cinema–but the more frequent and lurid application was in socialist rhetoric that represented capitalists as "bloodsucking" predators. Karl Marx's *Das Kapital* (1869; French tr. 1873; English tr. as *Capital*) makes continual reference to proprietors as "vampires."

Nizet gives no clear evidence of being a revolutionary socialist, in spite of being fervently anti-aristocratic and pro-proletarian, but Ion Heliade Radulescu had played a leading role in the local version of the wave of revolutions that swept Europe in 1848, and his daughters would certainly have been familiar with contemporary revolutionary rhetoric. This influence could have combined with that of *La ville vampire* to make it seem very appropriate to Nizet to symbolize the ultimate Russian bogey-man as an aristocratic vampire.

Before reading *Le Capitaine Vampire* the reader might find it useful to know a little more about the historical background of the story. The Ottoman Empire had been in decline throughout the 19th century, and its grip on its European components was seriously weakened once the revolutionary movements of 1848 had kick-started nationalistic independence movements in many of the relevant territories–especially those which had substantial Christian populations. Freedom of religious observation became a key demand of many of these movements, and licensed the intrusion of Western European nations, which could pose as champions of Christendom in lending support to anti-Ottoman activity. Whatever quantum of sincerity here may have been in the governments of France and Britain taking this line, however, there is no doubt that the Tsar of Russia was entirely concerned with the possibility of extending his own empire at the expense of the ailing Austro-Hungarian and Ottoman Empires.

Unlike the far-flung empires of France and Britain, the Russian Empire had always been geographically connected, expanding by annexation rather than by maritime adventurism. In this respect, the youngest and most aggressive imperial power in Europe, Otto von Bismarck's Germany, was something of a hybrid, but it too had political aspirations in Eastern Europe, which required delicate negotiations with the Russians regarding the pickings that might soon become available.

The Treaty of Paris, which ended the Crimean War in 1856, guaranteed the integrity of Turkey, which kept control of the provinces south of the Danube river. Russia, having been defeated, ceded Bessarabia, and the Black Sea was established as neutral. This accord did not last long, though; the Black Sea clauses were repudiated by a conference of the great powers that took place in London in March 1871, shortly after the armistice that brought the Franco-Prussian War to an end and shortly before the Peace of Frankfurt, by which France ceded Alsace-Lorraine to Germany. In September 1872, the Emperors of Germany, Austro-Hungary and Russia met in Berlin to negotiate an *entente*, which bound them to set aside their own disputes in order to present a united front against the Turks. This became a formal alliance in October 1873.

These political shifts greatly encouraged the revolutionary movements in the Ottoman sphere of influence, and the Sultan of Turkey was forced to promise reforms in December 1873. The Ottoman Empire was in desperate straits economically, high-interest bonds it had issued in order to raise revenues from western Europe having collapsed in value.[3] The promised reforms did not take place–not, at least, rapidly enough to satisfy the rebels– and the Turks became increasingly repressive; in one notorious incident in March 1876, their troops slaughtered Bulgarians on a massive scale.

This prompted the German/Russian/Austro-Hungarian alliance to issue the Berlin Memorandum of May 13, demanding that the Turks call a cease-fire and return to the path of reform (the British prime minister, Benjamin Disraeli, was invited to sign it, but declined– he too was apprehensive of the alliance). The Sultan of Turkey, Abdul Aziz, was assassinated on May 30, and several more members of the Ottoman government were murdered in June. On June 30, Serbian nationalists declared war on Turkey.

Abdul Aziz's successor, Murad V, was deposed on August 31, allegedly on the grounds of insanity. On October 31, the Turks agreed to an armistice in response to a Russian ultimatum, but Russia immediately began preparing to go to war against them. The Constantinople Conference in December ended in the proclamation of an Ottoman Constitution, which established parliamentary government and guaranteed freedom of worship, but the revolutionary tide had become unstoppable.

The Russians signed a formal treaty with the Austro-Hungarians in January 1877, permitting the latter to occupy Bosnia and Herzegovina in return for a free hand further east. Turkey and Serbia signed a peace treaty in February, but that could not prevent the Russians declaring war on April 24. The Russians immediately invaded Rumania, posing as liberators rather than conquerors, and absorbed the Rumanian army before crossing the Danube on June 27.

After taking several towns quite easily, the Russians began to suffer reverses in July and, eventually, became bogged down while besieging Pleven in August. It was in the course of that siege that it became imperative to capture a key item in Pleven's defenses, the Gravitza (or Grivitza) redoubt–and in order to achieve that aim, the Russian generals decided to use Rumanian troops to mount the first attack, which would undoubtedly result in very heavy casualties. In effect, the Russians ruthlessly and callously sacrificed their supposed allies in order to conserve their own strength–that, at least, was the way that Ion Heliade Radulescu's indignant daughters presented the event to their friend Marie Nizet, thus inspiring her to write *Le Capitaine Vampire*. In the novella, the insidious guiding spirit of Russia military conduct is Colonel Boris Liatoukine, nicknamed–perhaps deservedly–"Captain Vampire."

Two of the characters featured in Nizet's novella are based on actual individuals involved in the siege of Pleven, although she makes slight precautionary changes in their names. The actual General Cernat becomes the fictitious General Cerneanu and the actual General Angelescu (who was not promoted to that rank until after September 11, 1877) becomes Colonel Leganescu. The name of Androcles Comanescu also appears to have been adapted from that of one the Rumanian generals active in the campaign, Achille Comaneanu, although the fictional character has nothing at all in common with the actual person.

This translation has been made directly from a photocopy of the 1879 edition, which appears to be identical–save for a few typos–to the version reprinted by Matei Cazacu in 2004.

Brian Stableford

# CAPTAIN VAMPIRE

## *I. The Insult*

It was May 1877. The Russians were descending like locusts upon the magnificent country of Rumania, which had been surrendered to them as prey. The population of Iasi had quadrupled; troops were cluttering the railway lines and the Cossacks were invading Bucharest, despite a specific clause in the Rumanian treaty forbidding the imperial battalions access to the capital.

One hot afternoon, a number of peasants were sowing maize and barley in the vicinity of Bucharest. It is impossible for Rumanians to remain silent for an instant, and there was no lack of topics of conversation.

"They have no respect for anything!" said one young man, shaking his long hair. "They trample the corn, break our ploughs and burn our trees like dead wood! God only knows what they won't do!"

"And then, we have to give them lodging!" said another.

"Right, Mitica," said a third to the first speaker. "It wouldn't be so bad if they didn't drink so much!"

"I have my sister to consider," Mitica Slobozianu replied, simply.

An old man with a white beard–a stereotypical *eternal father*–doffed his sheepskin cap respectfully and said, in a grave voice: "If Heliade [4] had lived, they wouldn't have got past Ungeny."

"Old Mani's right," the peasants said, "but it's not a good idea to remember Heliade just now."

Old Mani Isacescu paid them no heed, and said with a sigh: "Heliade! I knew him. Those were good times."

Alas, the good times are always those that are long gone.

"Our father Bismarck, who art in Varzin..." [5] Mitica intoned, nasally. "Bah! We'll have plenty of things to ask of *our father Bismarck*, of which he won't grant a single one."

"You seem very cheerful, Mitica–thanks to the *raki*?" [6] insinuated one of the peasants.

Mitica blushed. "Don't spoil my good mood," he sighed, ceasing to smile. "It'll go away by itself soon enough. Next Sunday I've got to go to the town hall–where, depending on how unlucky I am, I'll either be enrolled in the territorial army or the regular army. They'll cut off my hair, while I wait to lose my head! There you go!" Passing his hand through his Merovingian locks, he added: "It's a shame, though."

"To the town hall!" the peasants exclaimed, unpleasantly surprised.

"Yes–like everyone else unfortunate enough to have been born in the year of our Lord 1856."

A cry of anger erupted from every bosom.

"And suppose we don't want to!" Manoli said, with a gesture of defiance.

"Well, your wishes will be overruled," Mitica replied, the *raki* having reconciled him somewhat to his fate. "To war, my friends, to war! If the Turks take us prisoner, they'll cut off our arms and legs. That'll be very amusing."

"And my son?" cried Old Mani. "What will they do with my son?"

"Your son? My God protect him–and all the other *dorobantzi*.[7] Isn't he coming back today? Well, since he's a corporal, he must know a lot more than me, a humble conscript."

Old Mani did not reply. He turned away and resumed throwing maize to the wind.

"They'll send us to Dobruja," Mitica continued, with an ironic verve that excited his companions. "We'll sleep in the marshes with the toads and eat *mamaliga* made with plaster–that's good enough for poor devils like us."[8]

"What are you doing, father?" a familiar voice suddenly put in, causing the old man to shiver. "You're sowing corn for the foreigners and preparing straw for their horses!"

"Ioan, my Ioan!" cried Old Mani, hurling himself upon his son.

"Isacescu!" said the peasants, immediately forming a circle around he soldier, as avid as could be to hear the lie given to the bad news brought by Mitica. Alas, the *dorobantz* could only confirm it.

Furious and exasperated, the peasants abandoned their work and took to their heels along the road, in the opposite direction to Bucharest.

"Say nothing to the women!" Ioan shouted after them.

Mitica and the *dorobantz* exchanged a few words.

"Are you going to Bucharest?" Ioan asked.

"And then I'll come back here," Mitica said. He added, with a smile: "Mariora's waiting for you."

"Poor Mariora!" sighed the *dorobantz*.

Mitica put his finger to his lips to command silence. Ioan made a sign to show that he understood, and remained alone with his father while his friend, whose robust cheerfulness was indestructible, went away whistling.

Ioan Isacescu appeared to be 22 or 23 years of age. He displayed all the distinctive features of his race; even if he had not been wearing the strange uniform of the *dorobantzi*, the slender and elegant figure, the olive complexion, the curly black hair descending over his forehead and–above all–the dark and profound eyes whose glare was unsoftened by their extremely long lashes, would have drawn from any Serb, Russian, Bulgar or Hungarian the possibly hostile and disdainful exclamation: "There's a Rumanian!"

The shadow of a moustache stamped his upper lip. The sole fault that an artist would have found with his face, which was otherwise perfectly handsome, was the extraordinary thickness of the eyebrows, which were almost joined together, and which lent his intelligent and pensive physiognomy a hint of wildness.

"Isacescu is proud!" said young women offended by the indifference of the *dorobantz*, who spared them neither a glance nor a friendly word. My God, no! Perhaps Isacescu's character was a little too serious, but he was certainly scornful of no one, and it was a cherished privilege to have him as a friend. In the territorial army, of which he was a member, the soldiers spent alternate periods of three weeks in their hearths and a week with their regiment. Old Mani Isacescu's flourishing fields gave scarcely any evidence of the brief absences of Ioan–who had succeeded, by means of his activity and economy, in doubling the little capital they possessed. Even his meager wages were put into his father's hands in full, and it was said that, although the Isacescus were not rich, they had a chance of becoming so.

The *dorobantz*, although brave to the point of temerity, hated boasting, and his horror of what one might call *staginess* had played a strange part in determining his future.

It was in 1876, at the time of the thaw. The Dimbovitza flooded the poor districts in the south of Bucharest and a great number of peasants, including Isacescu, had hastened to see the disaster. A pretty young girl of 16– who had not read Schiller's *Diver* [9]–threw a flower into the river and challenged the young men to go after it. They immediately threw themselves into the muddy water like a flock of geese, to the great delight of the pretty girl, who laughed at the sight of them splashing about, trying to get the better of one another. Although he had heard the imprudent words of his neighbor, whom he had known since childhood, Ioan remained where he was on the bank. His severe gaze met the little fool's eyes, and she blushed. From that moment on, she loved Isacescu. At first, Ioan's response to that affection, so bizarrely originated, was lukewarm; he allowed himself to be adored by the young woman as a Hindu god by a Brahmin. One day, though, he was astonished to find that he loved Mariora Slobozianu, if not more, then at least in an altogether different fashion to the manner in which she loved him.

Old Mani leaned on his son's arm; they left the sun-drenched plain. The maize would certainly yield a double harvest this year. But the two Isacescus were not thinking about maize!

They went along a narrow sunken path, bordered on either side by bushes and trees whose roots projected from the earth, and they chatted as they walked.

"The country's independence will be declared within the week," Ioan said. "They'll have us fire our cannons, then they'll pack us off to Giurgiu." With a smile, he added: "Probably with a double ration of *sel-bovitza*."[10]

"Giurgiu!" said Old Mani. "Giurgiu's on the Danube!"

"Yes, it's on the Danube–the right bank. They don't want to tell us because they fear a mutiny, but we've figured it out." After a pause, he continued in a lower voice: "Father, when I'm gone, you'll go to see Mariora from time to time, won't you? I'll simply tell her that we're going to garrison Giurgiu–she doesn't know that Giurgiu's on the Danube, so don't tell her!"

Old Mani replied with a nod of his head, his black eyes gleaming beneath his white eyebrows. He pointed towards Bucharest and pronounced, in a loud voice, the malediction that the Rumanian people consider irrevocable: "*A curse be upon them, their dead ancestors and their unborn children.*"

The arm he had raised to issue the curse remained outstretched. Ioan shivered, and suddenly lowered himself to the ground, setting his ear against it. The father and the son listened. A dull rumble reached their ears, similar to the steady gallop of a troop of horses.

"What's that?" the father asked.

"I don't know," the son replied. "It might be a cavalry unit passing by!"

The noise grew louder.

"They're horses," murmured Ioan, still leaning down to the ground. "Russian horses–I recognize their trot."

"Russians?" Mani repeated. "Which way are they headed?"

The *dorobantz* pricked his ears more attentively.

"Northwards," he said, finally. "They're coming towards us."

Scarcely had he pronounced these words when they saw a horseman appear a few hundred yards away, at the end of the path they were following–then another, and a third: an entire unit, as Ioan had said.

"Well?" said Old Mani, interrogatively.

"They're Cossacks, headed by a Colonel," said the younger Isacescu, whose eyesight had been honed on the streets. He was not mistaken; the Cossacks were coming down the sloping path at full speed.

"Let's get out of the way, father," Ioan said. "Here they are!"

The Russians had arrived within the range of an ordinary voice. The Colonel in command of them, having seen the two Walachians, cried out in strongly-accented Rumanian: "*Loc! Facetzi loc!*"–meaning "Give way! Get out of the way!"

The command was futile. The two Isacescus had their backs to a bank that was like a wall of earth. The Russians were riding three abreast, coming like the wind, and the path was no more than ten feet wide.

"*Loc!*" repeated the officer. "*Loc!*"

They could not go back any further. Ioan was about to reply when his eyes met the sallow face of the Russian Colonel. His terrible eyebrows frowned; he had just perceived a mocking smile in the greenish eyes of the officer, who was still howling: "*Loc! Loc!*"

The Colonel aimed his horse at the two Rumanians and shouted ferociously at old Mani: "Since when does a serf keep his cap on his head before a boyar?" With a rapid gesture, he lashed out with a slender horsewhip, which passed across the old man's forehead like a light-ning bolt.

Bursts of laughter sounded behind the insulter; a cry of rage replied to them. Ioan, pale with wrath and brandishing his dagger, threw himself at the horse's head. He seized the bridle with his left hand, and was about to strike its rider with his right, when the latter abruptly pulled away and drew his sword.

The saber came down violently upon the hand of the *dorobantz*; a jet of blood sprang forth, but the dagger remained firm in Ioab's iron grip.

If the Walachian was strong, the Russian was skillful. Releasing a guttural exclamation, he jammed his spurs into the flank of his chestnut horse, which set off at a gallop, dragging the *dorobantz*–who fell, bleeding, beneath the hooves of the Cossack horses.

When he got up again, Old Mani was by his side. Ioan looked around, with a strange expression; blood was dripping from his fingers, reddening the grass, but he did not feel the wound. He only saw his father, knowing and understanding but one thing: his adversary was out of reach! He calmly folded his arms across his chest and watched the Russians recede towards the horizon.

When the last soldier had disappeared from view, and the sound of the last horseshoe striking the ground had ceased to echo in his ears, he murmured in a dull voice: "For what you have just done, man with the yellow eyes–what you did to my father, and what you did to me–I swear, here before God, to repay you a hundred times over!"

## II. What Boris Liatoukine Was

That same May evening, a joyful sound of conversation and clinking glasses leaked out of one of the rooms in the Hugues Hotel, the most aristocratic in Bucharest. A crowd of young Russian officers, who had come straight from Iasi, were disporting themselves there.

The floor was strewn with the shards of broken bottles; merely by the manner in which these amiable young men downed the glasses of Rumanian wine that they were served, they were recognizable as Muscovites. The open windows gave passage to clouds of tobacco smoke and dozens of corks, with which the officers took pleasure in bombarding innocent passers-by.

"Who cares?" said Yuri Levine. "It's nice here! There are trees–which are in leaf, as in St Petersburg. I've always liked trees and leaves." The young Hussar seemed to be endowed with a sensibility that was quite rare among persons of his sort.

"Well, that's a fine thing to say at Countess M***'s ball!" exclaimed a tall fellow, whose name was Bogomil Tchestakoff. "Personally, I could never stand *green foliage and cool shade*, as my venerable aunt would put it– she has literary pretensions and claims that my aversion to nature is evidence of a moist throat and a desiccated heart." He drained the contents of his glass in one gulp. "These Walachians produce excellent wines!"

"Same goes for these little pastries," added a fat Pole, whose mouth was full. "They're very strong on little pastries."

"So you reckon, Bogomil," put in one Stenka Sokolich, who appeared to belong to the order of wading birds, "that we ought to exert ourselves to stay here for as long as possible?"

"Archduke Nicolas will see to that," said Bogomil, winking, "thanks to the pretty ladies..."

"Oh, the women are another thing!" cried Igor Moïleff, a sort of Petersburgian Don Juan. "They have primitive virtues, these little Dacian girls!"

"Oh, have you been tempted?" asked the Pole, with a loud laugh that he took pains to make dirty.

"Oh yes!" sighed Igor, negligently. "What else is there to do in an occupied city? And believe it or not, I was rebuffed–for the first time!"

"The first time, eh?" cried Stenka Sokolich. "And the Princess Sarolta K***, who..."

"She was an Ambassadress," Igor interrupted, impatiently. "I don't count Ambassadresses, myself."

"Oh, don't get upset–we believe you. Tell us your story instead."

Igor leaned back lazily in his armchair, lit a cigar and began: "This morning, I was innocently taking a stroll along what these good Walachians call the Chaussée–which I, personally, call 'under the lime-trees'–when I noticed a girl trotting along in front of me, whose figure didn't displease me and who seemed to be young. I could tell from her clothes that she was no boyar, so, assuming that things would be easy, I increased my pace. 'Mademoiselle,' I said to her, in French. She turned around. She wasn't exactly ugly, although she was as dark as a chestnut! She looked at me with fearful eyes, murmured a few words in that diabolical lingo they jabber hereabouts, and turned her heels towards me with no further ceremony. I fell into step with her. 'Mademoiselle,' I said again–and I summoned the assistance of my multilingual expertise–'*ia lioubliou tebia! ich liebe dich! io t'amo!*' Oh, but in vain–Russian, German and Italian were equally futile. She was deaf! In Petersburg or Berlin, a girl of her sort would have understood me even if I were speaking Chinese! I was wary of approaching too closely–she was escorted by an enormous dog that was looking at me sideways. I took the risk, though–and the beast opened its eyes! I wanted to talk to the beauty, not the dog. 'Muscha!' she said, suddenly. As I went to take her hand, the dog pounced–I had to let go, damn it. She didn't bear me a grudge, though–as soon as she got away from me, she called off her Cerberus, just as it was about to devour me."

"Bah!" said Bogomil Tchestakoff, "Liatoukine, who has exceedingly beautiful relatives here, will find us some palace where the cellars are well-stocked and the girls pretty. He's an invaluable man!"

"So where is Liatoukine, then?" they exclaimed, in chorus.

The emphasis with which they pronounced the name allowed the inference that Liatoukine was, at the least, a sufficiently important person not to cause well-born men to blush.

"You know very well that Liatoukine is everywhere," said Yuri Levine. "He has the gift of ubiquity, just like the good God of Archimandrite Samourkas-soff."

"Bah! Since I've been with the regiment I've heard no stories of any other sort," said Bogomil. "I've grown tired of it. Do you believe such tales, the rest of you?"

No," said Sokolich, whose Mephistophelean profile advertised his skepticism. "Despite his funereal aspect, I take Boris Liatoukine for an honest fellow, no more stained by Diabolism than this stout Pole here. Except that this is what a trustworthy old officer told me:

"It was in the Crimea. Remember that Liatoukine is older than us, and over 45. Liatoukine was in command of a Cossack regiment. You know that he doesn't have a soft heart. All Cossacks are thick-skinned, it's true, but Liatoukine plied the knout so often and hard that one day, when he found himself in an out-of-the way spot with his men, they stripped him naked, intending to freeze him to death–yes, freeze him to death! The funny thing is that Liatoukine didn't make a move to defend himself. On the contrary, he smiled. Water cascaded down on him, and when he had the appearance of a pretty crystal statue, the Cossacks, glad to be rid of their Lieutenant, got back on their horses. When they arrived back at camp, the first person they saw was Liatoukine, fully dressed and not even chilly. One of the Cossacks went mad, and Liatoukine had the rest–who would surely have died of fright without his intervention–executed by a firing-squad. Ever since then, he's been known in the army as *Captain Vampire*–a nickname he's kept even though he's now a Colonel."

Bogomil and the Pole burst out laughing.

"That's not all," Sokolich went on. "You know that Liatoukine has the reputation of being a lucky man. One evening–it was last winter, I believe–little Count M*** went back to his estate. A charitable friend was waiting at the railway station to tell him that Countess Malgorzata had gone to the theater with Liatoukine. Bad news! The Count ran to the Opera House; Malgorzata was there, in the flesh, with Captain Vampire at her side! M***, afraid of a scandal, swallowed his rage with his supper, but first thing the next morning, he presented himself at Boris's lodgings–where he was astonished to discover a companion in misfortune! Prince S***, whom you all know, was saying: 'Don't try to excuse yourself, sir! Yesterday, as Saint Isaac's chimed midnight, you were found in intimate company with the Princess!'

" 'You're mistaken, my Prince!' cried the bewildered M***. 'It was my wife that the gentleman took to the Opera; I saw them, as midnight sounded at the station.' And they started bickering. 'It's me!–no, it's me!–it's me!' A fine subject for discussion! Liatoukine, profiting from this altercation, refrained from clarifying the issue, and do you know how it finished? The two husbands fought a duel against one another!"

This Rabelaisian anecdote excited a general hilarity. The officers let loose that good Homeric laughter, which has suffered so much abuse from romancers, and which never sounds so well as when it bursts out at someone else's expense.

"Isn't it said that he's been married?" asked Boleslas Brzeminski.

"Twice over!" said Stenka Sokolich, who could have compiled the chronicles of St Petersburg's scandals. "His first wife was a tall, stiff Pole–one week of marriage and *crack!*–no more Princess Liatoukine."

"She died?" asked Brzeminski, who was not quick on the uptake.

"Absolutely. The second was more durable–that one lasted a month. One fine morning, all St Petersburg learned that Liatoukine was a widower once again. It was whispered abroad that the two women had been strangled and that they both bore a little red mark on the neck–the vampire's teeth, you know..."

"Damn! That makes the blood run cold!" said the Pole, only half-jokingly.

It is unnecessary to add that several more bottles had been drained to the last drop during Sokolich's story.

"So he isn't coming, then, dear Boris!" cried Bogomil, yanking the cord of a bell despairingly.

A waiter appeared. "What do your lordships desire?" he said, speaking French with a Hungarian accent.

"Liatoukine, my friend! Yes, we've lost him, and we'd dearly like to find him again," said Bogomil, shifting in his chair.

"But..."

"No buts, my lad! We need Liatoukine–he's a Russian boyar. Find him!"

"It's just that there are a great many Russian boyars here now," the waiter replied, with a tentative smile.

"Ah!" said Sokolic, smoothing down his moustache with his thumb. "Does that displease you, perchance?"

And they repeated, in various tones: "Liatoukine–we want Liatoukine!"

"Here he is, gentlemen!" said a voice that caused them all to start, as if impelled by a spring.

Liatoukine was standing in front of them.

As Sokolich had said, the newcomer had a funereal aspect. He realized, with surprising exactitude, the legendary type-specimen of the Slavic vampire. His figure, unusually long and thin, projected an enormous shadow behind him, which merged with the darkness of the ceiling. With a gesture redolent with a slightly cold dignity, he offered a fleshless hand charged with rings to the young officers, and deigned to take the seat that was respectfully offered to him. His hair and beard, which were intensely black, made the livid pallor of his long face stand out, its stern and glacial lines seeming more reminiscent of a marble monument than any human physiognomy. The soldiers had nicknamed him "Captain Vampire;" a stronger mind might have labeled him a *perfect gentleman*. The eyes, which seemed the only living things in that impassive face, displayed a singular feature: each eyeball, iridescent as a topaz, had a vertically slit pupil, such as one observes in animals of the feline family. The power of that gaze was such that no one could sustain it.

The ladies of Petersburg said that Liatoukine had the evil eye, and hastened to touch iron when he approached.

Liatoukine spoke sparingly. His voice had a metallic quality, which served him marvelously well in battle, but which resonated strangely in a drawing-room. No one had ever seen him laugh, and when he smiled, his features took on an expression of ferocity to which his oldest friends had not yet become accustomed. He had received a precious gift of nature, which his comrades envied him: that of drinking wine as others drank water. A large amethyst which he wore on his finger prevented him, they were convinced, from getting drunk. Having a great deal of influence, he had few declared enemies; his town house in St Petersburg was a customary meeting-place for Ministers and Ambassadors. He had published a highly-esteemed treatise on strategy, and the Tsar sometimes sent him on missions to Vienna, London or Berlin. To sum up, Captain Vampire was an officer of great valor; he had distinguished himself in the Crimea and Khiva, and Archduke Nicolas's staff officers whispered that he would be a General before the campaign ended.

As to the rest, his life was shrouded in mystery, and no one knew any more than Stenka Sokolich.

A witness would have been struck by the change that Liatoukine's presence had brought to the manner in which these young hotheads expressed themselves. *That dear Boris* had become *Colonel*; familiarity had been transformed into deference.

Liatoukine slowly drained a large glass of Cotnar wine, and surveyed his companions with his mesmeric gaze. "Gentlemen," he said, in his sonorous voice, "the boyar Androcles Comanescu has done us the honor of inviting us to the party that he is giving at 11 p.m. in his palace in the Strada Mogosoi. Ten o'clock has just sounded; we have time enough."

Liatoukine got to his feet, as stiffly as an automaton. The young men bowed and followed the Colonel, very happy to be able, at last, to parade their graces before the eyes of Rumanian ladies, which they promised themselves to dazzle.

Yuri Levine and the Pole formed the rearguard.

"He's very generous, this Cococescu!" muttered Boleslas, starting off by mangling the name of his Amphitryon.

"Shut up!" said Yuri. And, taking Brzeminski by the arm, he picked up Liatoukine's glass in his gloved fingertips. "Look!" he said holding the glass up to the lamplight.

"Pooh!" said the Pole.

And Yuri threw the glass out of the window.

## III. Mariora

Four or five miles from Bucharest, on the far side of the Baniassa Woods, a little white house stood in the middle of a tiny garden. The garden, where various plants vied to outgrow one another, was very narrow. The tile-roofed house seemed to be smiling through its small white-curtained windows. It all had an air of cleanliness and grace–which is not rare in Rumania, whatever people might say. Travelers halted instinctively in front of this cheerful habitation, and those who asked about the owners were informed: "They're the children of the late parish priest: the Slobozianus, Mitica and Mariora." And if the superb maize-fields round about caught their eyes: "Those are the Slobozianus' too–for as far as the eye can see, everything belongs to the Slobozianus."

While the Russians whom we have just left were drinking strong Cotnar wine and painting their friend Liatoukine in the darkest of colors, five or six young Rumanian women were gathered in the garden of the children of the parish priest. Some among them qualified as beauties, and none was straightforwardly ugly. They all wore the magnificent national costume, which retains echoes of Italy. Their double aprons of multicolored wool, the Byzantine embroideries that decorated their silken sleeves and the gold Turkish coins that shone in their brunette hair–invariably gathered into a thick plait–testified that they belonged to the families of wealthy peasants.

A joyful babble emerged from this pretty company. To tell the truth, they were gossiping about their neighbors, as people do in every village in the world when evening approaches–and God knows how Moldo-Walachian tongues wag!

"These Russians!" said a tall young woman of 20. "They think we're their slaves and they have a right to offend us."

"Zinca got married yesterday," said another. "They tried to carry off the husband."

"Bah! They couldn't carry off anything large." A loud burst of laughter greeted these words. Addressing a young woman whose clothes seemed slightly coarser than those of her companions and whose jet-black hair only bore red ribbons faded with wear, the speaker went on: "What did you say to the bold stranger?"

"Me? Nothing," said the young woman in red ribbons. "I didn't even understand what he said. I walked faster, that's all. In any case, I had my dog, which would have defended me."

"She's a savage, that Zamfira!" exclaimed Ralitza, a brunette.

"I hate the Russians!" murmured the one who had just been addressed as Zamfira.

"No," said the daughter of a wealthy farmer. "Zamfira's just faithful."

"Oh, faithful! Has the little one got a fiancé, then? Is it Stanciù the blacksmith or Stroïtza with the dancing bear?"

Zamfira blushed and made no reply, but a tear trembled on her eyelashes.

"One can't put on a show of being difficult when one has gypsy blood in one's veins," Ralitza put in. "Who wants a gypsy for a wife?"

"I know someone," said the oldest of the group, "and I forbid you to tease poor Zamfira–who's as good as you or me–any more."

Zamfira smiled and looked up, her eyes full of gratitude for her protector, who squeezed her hand gently.

"Was he handsome, at least, your Russian?" said Katinka, the farmer's wife.

"I don't know," Zamfira said. "I barely glanced at him."

"Ah! I would have known, myself," her interlocutor riposted. "Did he have black hair?"

"And yellow eyes?" said a soft and melodious voice from behind the young women.

The owner of the cottage, Mariora Slobozianu, had just appeared on the threshold.

Where are you, Rumanian poets too little known in the West–Heliade, Bolliaco, Alecsandri [11]–that you might tell us what a pretty thing this Mariora was?

Alecsandri would have cried, on seeing her: "Her hair is like the silvery rays of the Moon in summer, and her eyes recall the limpid mirror of a mountain lake!" Which, translated into vulgar language, signifies that Mariora had blonde hair and blue eyes.

She seemed, among her dark-complexioned companions, to be a daughter of the North astray beneath the serene skies of these southern climes–but her dainty feet, ever-ready to dance the *hora*, [12] her extravagant gaiety, bursting out on the slightest pretext, made her recognizable as an authentic Danubian. Her gaze had the calm profundity of the eyes of infants, and her smile was so sweet that it had finally captivated the heart of the wildest man in the neighborhood: Ioan Isacescu.

Mariora was leaning against the vine-clad wall, in a picturesque and slightly studied pose, the rays of the setting Sun brightening the vivid colors of her clothes, whose weave contained more threads of silk than strands of wool. Alas, the pretty Walachian had more than one fault. In all her life, not one serious thought had ever crossed her foolish mind, which was entirely occupied with the thousand trifles that have the privilege of delighting the sophisticated women of Paris and the female savages of Guinea to an equal extent.

Mariora was a coquette.

Her coquetry was fundamentally and entirely innocent; Mariora never dreamed of doing any harm and sought only to please Isacescu, whom she adored. She was considered by other young people to be a being of a superior kind; light conversation ceased when she approached, and she was held in respect as much on account of being the daughter of the late parish priest as the fiancée of the dreaded *dorobantz*.

Mariora was well-protected. She never went to Bucharest without the accompaniment of Baba Sophia, an aged female relative the priest had taken in, and the young boyars "returning from Paris" knew that anyone leaving the house of the sister risked meeting the brother's dagger or the fiancé's revolver at the corner. Only Lord Relia Comanescu, Mitica's foster-brother,[13] was admitted to the intimacy of the Slobozianu household; his mind was imbued with the caste prejudices of the previous century, and never even suspected that Mariora was pretty.

For her part, Mariora admired no one but Ioan Isacescu. He was poor, or nearly so, while she was rich; he possessed six miserable *pogones* [14] of land, while the Slobozianu estate covered an area of more than 50 hectares, all of which Mariora, an unconscious egoist, considered as her own property–a notion of which her brother, Mitica, did not think it necessary to disabuse her. Imperious and willful as she was, though, with regard to all those who surrounded her, a slight movement of the poor *dorobantz*'s eyebrows was sufficient to render her docile. Their wedding was to be celebrated within the year, although all the gossips in Baniassa were shaking their heads and muttering that, marriage or no, it would all end badly, and that Mariora was not the wife that Ioan Isacescu needed.

Perhaps that was true, alas. Mariora had the charming faults and caprices of a noble lady of Bucharest, which might prove rather embarrassing baggage beneath the roof of a simple peasant like Ioan. The wife of the parish priest–who had, incidentally, married beneath her–had devoted herself to educating her daughter in a plethora of small superfluous perfections, while neglecting to cultivate the solid qualities by means of which the young woman would easily have found employment in the position that she occupied. The end-result of this was that she had pretty pink fingers that did not know how to make cheese, and that she sang *doïne* [15] divinely, although it required more than courage to consume *mamaliga* that she had prepared. She seemed far less suitable for Isacescu's humble hearth than the sumptuous drawing-rooms of some boyar; she had long since confided the duties of her own household to Baba Sophia and Zamfira.

What was Zamfira? Oh, almost nothing. She and her father lived together in little hut they owed to the generosity of the Slobozianus. The father labored, sowed crops, weeded the garden and gathered the harvest on Mitica's behalf; he daughter helped–or, rather, replaced–

Mariora, and still found the time to weave nets and mats, which she sold in Bucharest. She was honest, according to supposition, although the question had scarcely been tested. She had had the misfortune to be born to a gypsy mother, thus suffering from a kind of proscription that may have struck her as unjust, but she never complained. She was very gentle, and when she wept, she was so quiet as to be scarcely audible. If Mariora was reckoned a pearl, Zamfira might have been called an angel.

Zamfira was devoted to Mariora; Mariora might have loved Zamfira if the gypsy had not had those poor frayed ribbons in her hair. There was a story attached to those ribbons, and they were the cause of Mariora frequently subjecting Zamfira to unmerited reproaches and wounding jeers. One day–it was about a year previously–Mitica had brought them back from the Mosilor fair, which is held in Bucharest during the week before Pentecost.

"Red!" the discontented Mariora had cried. "Why red, given that I'm blonde?"

Mitica smiled and did not reply. The following day, Zamfira appeared at the *hora* with the famous ribbons in her hair, to the great annoyance of Mademoiselle Slobozianu, who would not speak to her brother for a week, while complaining loudly that she did not want a Bohemian in the family. The continued sight of these ribbons exasperated Mariora, who set about making Zamfira into Danubian Cinderella; they had faded now, and Mariora had sworn that Mitica would not replace them.

Mitica Slobozianu loved Zamfira, not as the young men of Bucharest were habituated to loving gypsy girls, but in the manner that a brave and worthy girl–which is what she was–deserved to be loved.

Zamfira was not a beauty–her complexion, of a very pronounced bronze color, immediately revealed her suspect origin; her hair was as coarse as horsehair (Mariora called it prickly); she was short and two years older than Mitica–but such serene generosity was readable in her large black eyes that, on seeing her beside Mariora, people asked themselves whether the less pretty of the two might not be the more beautiful. Those eyes did not know how to lie.

"Why do you love Zamfira?" the young women said to Mitica. "She's neither pretty nor rich–and besides, she has pagan blood beneath her dark skin. A gypsy! They're old at 20!"

"I love her, first of all, because she loves me," he replied, simply, "and then because she's good–which can't be said of all of you, who have sharp tongues and empty heads."

Unfortunately, the tender affection that Mitica bore for Zamfira had not in the least diminished the young man's hearty appetite for *raki* and dancing.

Mariora's question regarding the Russian's eyes had caused her companions to shrug their shoulders.

"I thought it was only cats and owls that have yellow eyes," said Katinka the farmer's wife.

"Well, so much the better for you, my dear," said the priest's daughter, dryly. "There are things that it's better not to know."

"What do you mean?" cried the assembly, with one voice.

"I mean... I mean that I don't feel disposed to endure your aggravations this evening, and that you should have let me rest."

"Oh, I get it," said Ralitza, in a mocking tone. "The handsome Ioan Isacescu."

"It's Ioan all right!" Mariora murmured, ill-temperedly. Then, after a pause, she added: "Ioan! It's true—he'll come."

Something was evidently troubling her; her nervous fingers were twisting a sprig of box-wood from the hedge, and she was staring at the tips of her feet, presumably in order that her friends would not see the tears poised to escape from her eyes.

Florica, the raspberry-seller, begin to sing:

"*The yellow bird takes flight,*

"*Cleaving space with its beating wing;*

"*One might think it a golden arrow*

"*Flying overhead!*"

"*The Yellow Bird*–what a stupid song!" said Mariora. Who has ever seen a yellow bird cleaving space?"

This abrupt observation was exciting hilarity among the young women when Zamira, who had been searching the horizon with her eyes for some moments, put a hand on Mariora's shoulder and pointed to the Bucharest road, saying: "Ioan!"

Mariora shivered, and darted an anxious glance at the gypsy, while the playful group took flight, snatches of *The Yellow Bird* mingling with their bursts of laughter.

"Zamfira," Mariora said, suddenly, "I've told you nothing!"

Zamfira opened her mouth to reply, but Mariora was in her fiancé's arms and Cinderella slowly and reluctantly stole away.

As lithe as a cat, Mariora stood on tiptoe to match the *dorobantz*'s height and cover him with kisses. "You're very late!" she said to him, in a tone of gentle reproach, and drew him into the house.

Night was falling slowly, filling the corners of the room with shadows. "Baba Sophia!" the young woman shouted–but Baba Sophia was gossiping with some neighbor or other. Mariora had to light the enormous brass lamp–which was almost an object of luxury–herself.

While loading the table with eggs, fruits and a jug of *braga*,[16] which would comprise the couple's supper, Mariora babbled incessantly about God knows what. There were things that made no sense and meant anything at all, things that had been repeated since the world began and that people would never tire of hearing–except that the young woman did not seem to want to give Ioan time to reply. An attentive observer would have remarked that she was even seeking to avoid his gaze, which never left her.

Suddenly, she released a cry and seized Ioan's right hand. "What's that?" she exclaimed. "Blood! Are you hurt?" She lifted his blood-stained hand to her lips, while her eyes, full of anxiety, interrogated the *dorobantz*.

Ioan hesitated; he hated lying to her.

"It's a gunshot," he said, with an effort. "My rifle went off in my hands."

Mariora, who could not distinguish a wound made by a firearm from one made by a bladed weapon, did not perceive Isacescu's embarrassment. "Oh!" she cried, bathing the festering wound liberally. "Gunshots are dangerous! Almost as dangerous as going to war, no?"

"Not exactly," he said, forcing a smile that he tried in vain to make cheerful.

"War!" Mariora continued, pensively. Suddenly fearful, she added: "But there's war here. You'll never go to war, will you?"

"No," said Ioan. It was the second time he had lied.

"Because I wouldn't want that!" she cried, shaking her head in a mutinous fashion. "I need you, whatever this villainous Tsar that we don't know has done to us. Let him fight against the Padishah by himself, all alone. We have other things to do! Getting married, for example. When? Oh, the sooner the better, for I warn you that I'm getting tired of waiting. Aren't you?"

"Mariora!" he exclaimed. That was all he was able to say. There was both tenderness and reproach in his voice.

A few words from the innocent girl had reawakened the bitter thoughts that her caresses had lulled. Isacescu was thinking about the future, and about the insult he had suffered on the road–and a strange intermittent hallucination showed him his new enemy standing between himself and his fiancée. For a moment, he thought about telling her everything–his fateful encounter on the sunken road and his departure for Giurgiu–but they both had a secret, and Mariora said to him, in that slightly sulky fashion that she knew how to render charming:

"My handsome *dorobantz*, nothing can cheer you up today. Have you run into a *zmeu* [17] in the woods?"

"Yes," said Ioan, shuddering.

Mariora thought that he was joking. "What? Tell me about it, then," she said, smiling. "What does a *zmeu* look like? Does it have horns and wings, as Baba Sophia assures me?"

"No," said Ioan. "This one had yellow eyes and..."

"Yellow eyes!" Mariora interrupted, anxiously. "You've seen the man with yellow eyes?"

"Yes," Ioan replied, calmly. "And you've seen him too, apparently?"

"Me!" she cried, blushing. "Holy Mother of God, no! Are there really men with yellow eyes?" She plunged her hand into the soldier's thick hair and continued, murmuring like a turtle-dove: "I've never seen hair as fine as yours, Ionitza. It's so soft! It's lovely."

But Ioan remained insensible to these caresses; his apparent calm concealed a violent internal agitation.

Mariora saw Ioan's eyebrows quiver. "Oh, don't look at me like that!" she said, trying to pull away. "It makes me feel ill; there's too much black in your eyes."

"It's true that there's a great deal of black," he repeated, mechanically. There was a pause. Then he went on, coldly: "Mariora, has someone been here?"

"No one, my love, no one... except for the boyar Relia Comanescu." She added: "He was very boring; he talked about nothing but wine and maize."

"No one? Are you quite sure about that, Mariora?" The *dorobantz*'s features were contorted; his words, stamped with an unaccustomed hardness, frightened the priest's daughter.

"How you say that!" she cried. "Who do you think came?"

"A man with yellow eyes," Ioan said.

Mariora attempted a burst of laughter, which sounded so false even to her that she was terrified. She was about to reply when a voice sounded gravely in her ear, murmuring: "Mariora, it isn't right for you to hide something from your future husband."

It was Zamfira, who had just come in. Without taking any notice of her friend's angry start, she went to sit down on the other side of the room and silently set about weaving her rushes.

Mariora, red with shame, dissolved into tears.

"All right–yes, I'll tell you everything!" she sobbed. "Everything–on condition that you don't look at me while I speak!"

Ioan Isacescu would have accepted other conditions as well; he did not understand and made every effort not to want to understand. He was very pale, but he made an affirmative nod.

Mariora wiped her tears, sat down beside the *dorobantz* and put her arm around his neck. Then she looked at him timidly, as if she wanted to borrow a little courage from his loving eyes.

"This is what happened," she began, in a very low voice. "This morning, Zamfira and Baba Sophia went to Bucharest, leaving me alone here. All the men were in the fields. I wasn't doing anything–I was thinking about you!–when I heard the gallop of an approaching horse.

"I ran to the door, expecting to see the boyar Comanescu, whom we were expecting. It wasn't him; it was a Russian officer. He dismounted. I thought he wanted to speak to me and I went towards him. Oh, I shouldn't have gone towards him–but how could I know? Eventually, he pointed to his horse, which was panting, and said two words: 'water, horse.' The way he spoke, which was anything but polite, shocked me; nevertheless, I went to fetch water, assuming that he couldn't speak Rumanian very well. I was mistaken, Ioan–that man expresses himself better than an Oltu riverman! While the horse was drinking, I observed its master. Jesus Christ!"

Mariora went on: "If I live to be a hundred, I won't forget him! He was tall, so pale and thin that he could have been taken for a dead man. It seemed that I could hear his bones rattling–but what frightened me most of all was the yellow gleam in his round eyes. When the horse had finished, I turned to go back in; to my great astonishment, the man followed me. I told him that the house wasn't an inn. He replied that it was all the same to him and continued following me. I didn't dare say anything; there was a sepulchral tone in his voice that made me shudder. He sat down at the table as if he owned the place and ordered me abruptly to sit down in the chair opposite. I was terrified; I no longer knew what I was doing; I obeyed.

"He stared at me fixedly for about ten minutes. I had an urgent desire to run away, but I felt my strength diminishing–and I had noticed, besides, that he had set himself between me and the door. Finally, he got up. I got up too. His eyes never left me. He came towards me. I drew back, and kept going backwards–but the wall was there. I closed my eyes, for I had just felt a cold hand grip my arm–which had the same effect as if a snake had touched me.

"He picked me up, effortlessly, went back to his seat at the table, and sat me down on his knee, rudely. I was afraid of irritating him by futile resistance. 'Look at me,' he said.

"His will seemed to have become mine. I looked at him, just as he instructed–but, as his back as to the window, I could see men sowing barley in the distance, far away in the fields. It was to them that I looked for my salvation, but my screams wouldn't have been able to reach them. I told myself that the only thing that I could do was to put myself in God's hands and I prayed. The man didn't budge. But I couldn't pray for long; a strange numbness overwhelmed me by degrees. It seemed to me that I was falling asleep. I mustered the residue of my will-power to resist that drowsiness, which was bound to be my ruination, but I couldn't do it, and my dazed head soon lapsed on to the man's shoulder. Then..."

"Then?" Ioan broke in, in a strangled voice–and his fingers gripped Mariora's wrist with so much force that his nails sank into her flesh.

"Then," she said, "Relia Comanescu came in–I was saved!"

Laughing and crying at the same time, she buried her head in Ioan's bosom. "Ionitza, Ionitza!" she said.

He let her go. He looked at her with a strange smile. It was as if he had not seen her for some time, and was astonished to discover her in his arms. "Relia Comanescu!" he murmured. "Whatever danger he finds himself in, and whatever service he demands, that man may count on me!" He went on, immediately: "And Mitica? Where was he while this outrage was perpetrated upon his sister?"

A soft voice, which was more regretful than accusatory, sighed: "In Bucharest."

"In Bucharest? When his presence was required here?"

"He was dancing the *batuta* with his comrades," Zamfira went on, in utter confusion. "They had been drinking *raki*... perhaps a little too freely."

Ioan shrugged his shoulders and addressed Mariora. "Do you know this man's name?" he said.

"No. Comanescu appeared to know him; he pronounced his name two or three times, but they were speaking in a foreign language–and besides, I was so distressed that I couldn't take it in. *Ine*... It ended with *ine*, I think."

Ioan knew that one Russian name in four terminated thus. He made Mariora give him a detailed description of the Russian officer; the more she said, the more certain he became that his adversary of the sunken path and Mariora's insulter were one and the same.

"This man will bring disaster upon us!" said Mariora. As if frightened by her own words, she drew closer to Ioan, who repeated her words in a dull tone: "This man will bring disaster upon us."

"Heaven preserve us!" said Zamfira, moved by her superstitious pity to get up and light a candle in front of the sacred images.

Ioan Isacescu had scant faith in the power of candles, though. "Mariora," he said, suddenly, "Why did you want to conceal what had happened from me?"

The young woman had not been expecting such a question. She seemed to be embarrassed, and twisted the corner of her apron between her fingers.

"I don't know," she said, eventually. She was not lying this time. She did not know—but her reply did not satisfy Isacescu, whose features took on the painfully ironic expression that caused the girls of the neighborhood to say that the handsome dorobantz was not unfamiliar with the kind of *zmeine* [18] that are manifest as lovely female demons.

Mariora guessed what Ioan was thinking. "My love," she said, with dignity, "did you think my intention was to deceive you?"

Ioan's only reply was to take her by the hand.

"To deceive you!" she went on. "I shall be a long time dead before that shameful notion crosses my mind. To deceive *you!* If I were ever unfaithful, my handsome *dorobantz*"–she shook her head in a melancholy fashion–"would it hurt you very much?"

"Yes," said Ioan.

"Would you die of sorrow?"

"No," he said, firmly. "I'm stronger than sorrow."

"Ah!" Mariora formed a slight pout of disappointment, which might have had Ioan laugh on another occasion. "But you would surely kill me with your big sword–me, and the other!"

"You, no–the other, certainly."

"But what must you think of me, and the silly things I say!" she cried, all of a sudden. "Oh, pardon me! My poor head's aching and I no longer know what I'm saying from one moment to the next. There's one thing that terrifies me: that man, as he left, told me that I would see him again! I don't want to see him again!" She was speaking forcefully. "I'm frightened! You're coming back tomorrow, aren't you, Ionitza? You won't leave me again?" She added, in a murmur: "I think he'll come back!"

She clutched Ioan's clothing and fear was readable in her haggard eyes, which were staring into the void. "What will I do when you're not here?" she said.

"Not give any more water to strangers' horses," he replied, with a smile that calmed her.

"I won't leave you alone again," said Zamfira, making every effort to appear cheerful. "This terrible Cossack won't get the better of both of us!"

"Do you think so?" said Mariora, timorously.

Baba Sophia came in. Darkness had fallen. Ioan Isacescu said farewell to the two young women–and, while Mariora was pledging eternal amity to Zamfira for the thousandth time, the *dorobantz* walked away into the moonlight.

Instead of taking the path that led to Old Mani's hut, though, he took the road to Bucharest.

## IV. A Tragic Ball

The boyar Androcles Comanescu had supported every cause, belonged to all political parties and served every government. He was reputed to be one of the richest landowners in the country, and Domna Rosanda–a Serb who had brought a marvelous beauty, which was fortunate, as well as a considerable dowry, which was even better, to their marriage–had taken it into her head to make him a Senator. Comanescu, carefree by nature, let his ambitious wife have her way; she, with a view to the approaching elections, was already busy sending cartloads of *braga* to the neighboring villages, intended to make certain of the peasant vote.

Domna Rosanda was a masterful woman, to whose subtle influence the poor boyar was–so to speak–unconsciously submissive. Her maternal dream was to see her daughters shine at the Court in St Petersburg one day, and the noblewoman's avowed desire became, by degrees, the secret desire of her feeble spouse. Besides, it was not without a vague sentiment of pleasure that the boyar saw rough-mannered Cossacks circulating in the streets of Bucharest, and handsome Hussars laced up like maidens. Androcles–who, like others less naïve,[19] was readily led astray by seductive appearances–sincerely believed that he was acting patriotically in welcoming the Russians as liberators.

An opportunity to be agreeable to these new allies soon presented itself, and Comanescu was not prepared to let it escape him. A certain statesman, of short stature but immeasurable ambition, had given him to understand that it would be appropriate for some noble inhabitant of

51

Bucharest to organize a party, to which the principal Russian officers *passing through the capital* would be invited. Androcles had understood; under the pretext of following a suggestion, which was actually a disguised order, he yielded his palace to German upholsterers and decorators. A week later, high society, the staff of various embassies and the Russian officers *passing through the city* were crowded into the huge reception-rooms in the Strada Mogosai; Comanescu was giving a ball.

The Rumanian ladies were wearing dresses made in Paris, modified to suit the tastes of Bucharest—which is not the same thing as good taste. They were admirably beautiful, to be sure, these quasi-Oriental women, and the sight of them drew enthusiastic exclamations from the Russians, but how much lovelier they would have been if they had only been able to leave their family jewels—which sparkled in their hair, on their arms, in the pleats of their skirts, and even in the satin laces of their dancing-slippers—in their caskets!

Even the men seemed enamoured of jewelry, and their breasts proudly bore the insignia of more-or-less fantastic orders. Rumanians love everything that glitters, whether it be gold or gilded brass.

The ladies did the honors of their native land with perfect grace. They offered Turkish cigars to the foreigners with their dainty fingers, poured out Tokay such as Count Andrassy [20] never drank, and offered them rose jam made by nuns. Yuri Levine sighed with satisfaction; Boleslas, Stenka and Bogomil thought they had been transported into the Mohammedan paradise, and wanted to convert to Islam. Never had invaders been better received by the invaded. Everyone was speaking French, which is the aristocratic language of Rumania, and anyone who had had the untoward idea of pronouncing a few words in Rumanian would not have found a danc-ing-partner all night. Beneath the windows of the man-sion, however, the people were speaking the forbidden tongue. What were they saying? No one cared.

The principal Russian officers, among whose num-ber was the sinister Liatoukine, surrounded the little Minister, who hopped about and gesticulated with a typically Southern vivacity. His speech was so rapid that the guests, who were listening with a perseverance bor-dering on indiscretion, could only catch such phrases as *cross the Danube* and *Rumanian army*.

There was little dancing, much drinking and a great deal more talking. The gentlemen chatted about the is-sues of the *Romanul* [21] that they were reading in the window-bays; they commented on Rosetti's latest edito-rial, and the widely-remarked absence of the English Ambassador, who had made his excuses. The ladies, thinking that they were *being political*, offered excited critiques of the costumes of Princess Elisabeth, and one old noblewoman claimed that the ex-Prince Cusa had an even grander air about him than Prince Charles. Mali-cious tongue suggested that she was in a better position to know that than anyone else.

Domna Rosanda was triumphant. Her two daugh-ters, covered with gemstones, sparkled like sunbeams on the arms of their dancing-partners, who gave the impres-sion that they were not ignorant of the fact that they were dancing with millions. The Serbian had showered so much affection on the heads of Epistimia and Agapia that she had not enough to spare for her son, Relia, the sole male descendant of the illustrious family of Co-manescu.[22]

Relia–or, less familiarly, Aurelio–was little known in Bucharest. He was freshly-arrived from Paris, where he had shone but dimly in his studies. He was, all in all, a very gentle and timid boy, not Parisian at all, who professed a respect for his mother that was not far removed from dread. In the Latin Quarter, the way he had of lowering his gaze had earned him the nickname "*Mademoiselle Aurélie*."

Domna Agapia, who was scarcely 16, was already in search of a husband. Her brown hair, red lips, dazzlingly clear complexion–very rare in Rumanian cities–and little black eyes lively with malice made up a face that was attractive, despite the irregularity of its features, and had no lack of originality. Some thought her pretty, others thought her ugly; in truth, she was both at the same time. She had a way of chattering which might have passed for intelligence if the cheerfully plump girl had not posed as a sentimentalist. Furthermore, she was subject to caprices that were impossible to satisfy and fits of anger that made her rip her handkerchiefs and beat her chambermaids.

Domna Epistimia, who was pale, thin and lanky, replicated her mother's cold and correct beauty. She was a true Princess. There was no spontaneity in her. She had learned to think, to smile and to speak as she had learned to dance, to curtsey and to push back the train of her dress with a flick of her fan. Her voice, which she knew how to render sweet, was attractive; her gaze, intense and piercing, was off-putting. She was a creature of contrasts; beneath her satin skin and velvet skirts, she concealed a hard heart and a quarrelsome and calculating mind. She was not in the least stupid, in any respect, and knew how to conduct an intrigue.

By the time midnight drew near, Epstimia had succeeded in taking possession of Colonel Liatoukine and was promenading him majestically through the dense crowd of guests. The Rumanian was not talking; the Russian did not breathe a word. They passed like shadows, and the gallery observed that they had a great deal of *distinction*.

The Colonel's *distinction* had a slight smack of the cemetery. His pallid face took on a greenish tinge in the light of the chandeliers; his eyes, deep-set in their orbits, gleamed like an owl's, and the silver braid of his uniform, set in horizontal lines across his breast, gave him the false appearance, from a distance, of an ambulatory skeleton–which did not give the lie to the sinister rumors laid to his account.

Such as he was, Captain Vampire attracted the gazes of women, ever avid for mystery and violent emotion; more than one pretty noblewoman was jealous of Domna Epistimia.

Princess Agapia was monopolizing Igor Moïleff, whom she was bombarding with such questions as: "What flower do you like best? What's your favorite color? Do you prefer Turkish tobacco to Latakian, or black horses to bays?"

Igor replied, rather awkwardly, that his favorite plant was tobacco, that, as regards colors, he found *bay* enchanting, and that he never mounted any but Turkish horses. This did not prevent Agapia from finding him infinitely intelligent and his judgment very sound.

"Personally, she said, "I love sunsets, Chinese furniture, the song of the nightingale and vanilla cream, but I adore poetry." Putting on her best squint, she asked: "Do you like poetry, Monsieur?"

Igor could only reply affirmatively, and God knows whether he lied.

"Perhaps you *are* a poet?" the Princess suggested.

"Not as far as I know."

"One is sometimes one without knowing it," the plump Agapia sighed, lifting her eyes to the ceiling.

But this was not the case with Igor and the Princess resumed her own enumeration. "I love..." she said–and might have ended up confessing that the objects which partook of her affections included gilded epaulettes and fine moustaches, if she had not suddenly been made to turn around by a quivering movement imparted to her dress.

Boleslas Brzemirski was there, blushing with confusion, having caught his foot in the pink silk train that the Princess was dragging in her wake. He muttered a few unintelligible words. Agapia gave a slight nod of the head and gathered in her dress with dignity.

"Who is that officer walking with my sister over there by the buffet?" she asked Igor. "The pale one with the strange eyes?"

She was no longer paying attention to Boleslas, but the Pole came back from the buffet, where he had spent the entire evening. "Him?" he said, bowing more deeply than the young woman's age and rank required. "That's Captain Vampire!"

Agapia and several other ladies released little cries of fright.

"Yes, Mesdames," the Pole repeated. "That's Captain Vampire!"

Igor studied Brzemirski's luminous face and haggard eyes apprehensively. "Go back to the buffet," he whispered in his ear–but the Pole was not listening.

"As you can see, he's died and been resurrected at least three times."

"What nonsense!" said an Ambassadress.

A diabolical notion came into Boleslas' head. "Would you like Captain Vampire to tell you the story of his successive resurrections himself?" he asked.

"Certainly! That would be amusing!" cried Agapia– and before Igor could say a word to prevent him putting such a strange project into execution, Boleslas advanced upon Boris Liatoukine, in as straight a line as he could contrive, given the quantity of liquid he had absorbed.

Liatoukine saw him coming and smiled.

Liatoukine's smile was hideous, but what might have alarmed Count Brzemirski on an empty stomach scarcely intimidated the drunken Polish Hussar. Boleslas planted himself resolutely in front of his adversary, put his hands on is hips, and said, in a bantering tone: "Liatoukine, my good friend, they claim that you were frozen to death by your Cossacks at Sebastopol. Is that true?"

These singular words had been pronounced so loudly that the greater number of the people present heard them. Individual conversations immediately ceased and all eyes focused on the group formed by the two officers and Princess Epistimia.

The Pole, at the risk of losing his equilibrium, balanced himself on one leg and continued: "And that one day, you were found at the same time in company with Countess M*** and Princess S***. Is *that* true, eh?"

Liatoukine did not move, but he was no longer smiling. The expectant crowd held its breath.

The Pole went on again: "And that you've been married twice, that both your wives died within a month of marriage, and that they both had their necks wrung?"

Boris felt Epistimia's arm trembling upon his own. He, however, remained calm, and said in a clear and firm voice: "This man is drunk! Come away, Madame." He took a step to remove himself.

The Pole, with a single bound, pounced upon him.

"Ah! It must be true, Boris Liatoukine!" he cried, in a voice choked with anger. "There! There! Look, everyone!" His fingers brushed the Colonel's sleeve. "There's blood there!" He howled in exasperation: "Get away! You reek of murder and the tomb!"

Liatoukine did not even glance at his sleeve, and the large red stains there that had just been pointed out, with more astonishment than horror. He drew himself up to the full height of his tall frame in front of Brzemirski and his eyes stared into the enraged eyes of the Pole. The latter tried to speak, extended his clenched fists, and fell stiffly to the floor.

Then there was a general, every-man-for-himself panic.

Agapia screeched like a peacock and buried her head in Igor's epaulette. Epistimia let herself fall gracefully into Liatoukine's arms. Her example was followed by a great many ladies, who fell, according to their preference, upon the breasts of Russians and high dignitaries. A pretty Ambassadress ran partially aground upon an old Senator, while chance brought together two divorced spouses, who let chance have its way. Androcles Comanescu, who did not want to put himself at risk, stood aside and suggested *separating the combatants*. A Hungarian Countess demanded the police; Domna Rosanda, with greater foresight, sent for a doctor.

A few ladies, bolder than the rest, went to Brzemirski, who was lying unconscious on the floor, but as he was neither handsome nor interesting, they did not stay long. Relia went from one group to another, murmuring excuses, but it was hardly worth the trouble; the mothers did not want to hear and drew their daughters away.

The doorways were too narrow to allow the passage of everyone trying to leave; people pushed and jostled. The servants ran around agitatedly and the rumble of carriages carrying guests away was heard outside.

Prince G\*\*\*, who had claims to intelligence, put it about that it was a lot of fuss over a drunken Pole. The suggestion was not a success; the Prince seemed vexed and followed the crowd.

No one stayed in the immense and resplendent room except for Brzemirski's four friends and Domna Rosanda–who, still dressed in her ball-gown, was wasting her smelling-salts on Boleslas. The Oriental essences could do nothing, though. The Pole was dead.

Liatoukine had disappeared.

The officers looked at one another. They were all very pale.

"Apoplexy!" said Igor, to break the silence.

"No," said Sokolich. "It's something else."

"What, then?"

"Who can tell, damn it?"

Bogomil, the most strong-minded of the group, shrugged his shoulders. "He owed me 500 rubles," he moaned, mournfully.

Meanwhile, Domna Agapia was writhing in her bed like one possessed. "Dobry, Dobry! Light! Do you think I can remain in darkness when there's a dead man downstairs?"

The serving-woman withdrew, after bringing a perfumed candle, and Domna Agapia continued her lamentations. "That Pole," she sobbed, "has just died, in the middle of a ball, right in front of me, at my very feet! It'll make me ill, that's for sure! The other officer was very pleasant–yes, very pleasant! He reeked of wine–he was drunk, the lout! The other one had nice eyes... yes, blue eyes! Aren't they dirty, these Poles–ugly and ill-educated? Oh, I hate them; I curse them... yes! The other..."

"Shut up, Agapitza," said a muffled voice emanating from the next room. "One prays for the dead; one doesn't insult them!"

Agapitza, who had recognized her mother's voice, hastened to obey and went to sleep, still waving her closed fist threateningly at poor Brzemirski–who had not, however, done it on purpose.

Domna Rosanda, sitting next to her elder daughter's bed, said: "He has more than two million rubles."

Epistimia, who was propped up on her pillow smoking a cigarette, repeated "Two million rubles!" distractedly. Her eyes followed the smoke that was forming a sort of cloud above her brunette head.

In a room on the floor below, the four Russians watched over their friend's corpse.

By noon on the following day, all Bucharest had heard what had happened during the night. People started out by recounting the thing as it had occurred. Then, they said that the Pole was a rejected suitor who, in order to avenge himself, had committed suicide before the eyes of the insensible Epistimia. They finished up swearing that Brzemirski had been murdered by a Russian Colonel who was the Princess's fiancé. The last version, being the most exciting, was considered the only true one.

The Pole, who no longer had any family, was buried without ceremony in the Catholic cemetery on the Serban-Voda Road. With every day that passed, talk of his tragic end diminished, and the worthy tongues of Bucharest soon forgot his name.

## V. The Baniassa Woods

Independence! *Boom*! *Boom*! From the Ister to the Carpathians, Rumania was free! Cannon salvoes, fireworks, a speech by the Prince: the festivities lacked nothing–not even, this time, the enthusiasm of the people, for whom the government had sugared the pill, and who swallowed it with a very good grace.

The *raki* ran in torrents; in every country inn, the *babuta* and the *piper*–which was merely a frenzied can-can–ran their course, and–may God pardon me!–the Rumanians, in their gaiety, taught the Russians to dance the *hora* to the accompaniment of infernal gypsy music. Enormous seesaws, which bore no resemblance to those made for children, delighted the young women, lifting 20 people at a time and howling on their pivots. The streets were reminiscent of the galleries of an ant-hive. Along the Chaussée, the hubbub was indescribable. The Chaussée was a huge thoroughfare planted with lime-trees, which began in the fashion of the Champs-Elysée and ended in the manner of the Bois de Boulogne–except that, here, the Bois de Boulogne was called Baniassa. Elegant folk rarely went as far as Baniassa, whose promenade had fallen from grace and had been abandoned; they preferred the blinding dust of the interminable Chaussée to the outmoded shade of the woods.

This evening, the plebeian element had invaded the aristocratic domain, and the beautiful ladies, indolently extended in their Viennese carriages, made progress, less by virtue of being pulled by their horses as being pushed by the vulgar folk crowded into the interstices between the vehicles.

The Comanescus' emblazoned calèche proudly carried the Princesses Epistimia and Agapia, accompanied by their mother, who distributed charitable advice to them from time to time.

"Agapitza, my child, sit up straight–Decebale Privighetoriano is looking at you. Eight thousand hectares of agricultural land and property in Hungary."

Agapitza sat up, and put on a majestic air.

"Epistimia, my dear," the noble lady continued, "straighten your hair–what if the Colonel comes?"

Epistimia passed her white hand over her temples and darted a haughty glance at the surrounding crowd.

Meanwhile, Decebale Privighetoriano–pearl-grey gloves, pince-nez, Mexican trousers–sniggered in a friend's ear. "Look at that fat Agapia–built like a tavern-keeper! I'm told she weighs more than 80 kilos. I know a little actress at the Bossel theater who looks more like a Princess than that lumpen girl!"

No Colonel being on the horizon, Epistimia became impatient, and dug her pointed heels into her sister's feet; the latter had been too well brought-up to make the least grimace under the eyes of a boyar who owned 8,000 hectares of agricultural land. None of these three worldly souls spared a thought for Relia, whose fate–scarcely respectable–was to become a simple *dorobantz*, and who was leaving for Giurgiu within the hour.

Lost in the multitude, on foot, were Mariora and Ioan Isacescu, Zamfira and Mitica Slobozianu.

Zamfira had been weeping. Mitica wore the uniform of the *dorobantzi*, and his cheerfulness appeared to have stayed behind in Baniassa. Ioan was distraught. Mariora was the only one chattering in her usual fashion, not without an occasional sideways glance of annoyance at Mitica and the gypsy girl, who were speaking in hushed voices. Mariora could not hear what they were saying, which was a great pity.

"Giurgiu!" she said, laughing. "What an odd notion, their sending you to Giurgiu! Myself, I thought the *dorobantzi* never garrisoned any towns except those where they live."

"Not always," Ioan replied, fearful of saying too much.

"Will you be in Giurgiu for long?"

"I don't think so," he said, fiddling with his belt-buckle.

Mariora clapped her hands. "So much the better," she cried–but added, sadly: "I'll be very bored while you're away."

"Do you think so?" he said, with a half-smile.

Mariora released a deep sigh and lifted her eyes heavenwards.

"My father will come to see you often. He..."

"Your father! He's not you! That isn't the same thing at all!" she cried, blushing.

Ioan squeezed her small hand gently within his own, and they walked in silence for a little while.

"And we aren't married yet!" said Mariora, peevishly. "If we had been, I would have come with you to that nasty place, which I hate!" She went on, mysteriously: "Listen–I'm jealous of Giurgiu."

"Jealous? Of Giurgiu?"

"Yes–don't laugh. I'm jealous, and I have many promises to demand of you. So listen!" She slipped her arm under that of the *dorobantz*. "First, I want you to be bored as often as possible, so that you think about me all day long..."

"But if I think about you..."

Oh–that's true!" she said, smiling. "You won't be bored. So be it! I demand that you keep company with Mitica as little as you can, because Mitica..." She frowned, and added in a whisper: "It's the *raki*, you see!"

Ioan smiled, and attempted to speak.

"Wait–that's not all. You'll write to me every day–and you'll prevent Mitica from writing...to *her*."

"Mariora!" he exclaimed, in a reproachful tone.

"That's all right, isn't it?" she murmured, in a coaxing voice.

"No," said Ioan. "I can't do what you ask of me. Zamfira and Mitica love one another, just as we love one another. We'd draw the wrath of Heaven down upon us if we as much as thought of hurting them in such a cruel fashion. What would you say if your brother wanted...?"

Mariora guessed the rest of the sentence. Impatiently, she exclaimed, a little too loudly: "You're not a gypsy!"

"What's that?" said Mitica, whose head–entirely shorn of its long black locks–appeared over the young woman's shoulder.

"Nothing... nothing... I was talking about those gypsies over there, with their dancing bear."

Mitica enjoyed embarrassing his sister; an ironic smile played upon his lips. "Be careful, little sister," he said, significantly. Dropping back a few paces, he rejoined his companion.

"Mariora," said the *dorobantz*, "let's not talk about Mitica and Zamfira."

"Yes, let's not," she sighed. "They're very boring."

"Mariora," he continued, taking her by the hand without paying any heed to her abrupt remark, "there's something I've wanted to give you for some time... something that constantly reminds me of you."

"My Ionitza!"

"It's not of any great value," he went on, in a emotional voice, "but it was my mother's–she traveled a lot in her youth, as you know, and she brought it back from Constantinople..."

At that moment, Mariora felt something cold sliding along the length of one of her fingers. She withdrew her hand excitedly–and saw, to her surprise, a pretty ring that shone like gold.

The ring was made of copper. A jeweler would have laughed through his nose at anyone who wanted to sell it, but an antiquary would have thought himself lucky to be able to place it in his collection. Large enough to cover an entire knuckle, it was elaborately engraved; mingled with the Byzantine arabesques was a phrase in Greek or Turkish–Ioan could not tell which. The ring was worthy of attention by virtue of its strangeness; it was very old, and there was probably no other like it.

(I know that *the ring* is a hackneyed gesture, but, from Kamchatka to Senegal, fiancés have piously conserved its usage, and however it may displease the reader avid for novelty, Mariora received Ioan's copper ring joyfully.)

"It's pretty, Ionitza, it's pretty!" she repeated. "Is it gold?"

"I don't know," Ioan said, "but I don't think so."

"Yes, yes! I can see that it's gold!" insisted Mariora, who was a great believer in intrinsic value. "I'll never take it off–never, my Ionitza!" And, without worrying about what anyone might say, Mariora kissed the *dorobantz* in the middle of the Chaussée.

"In your turn, my beloved," Ioan said, "would you promise me...?"

"Anything you wish," Mariora interrupted, devouring her ring with her eyes. "Anything at all!"

Ioan Isacescu's features took on a wild expression. His famous eyebrows bristled and his hand went instinctively to his belt as if in search of the hilt of a dagger.

"Mariora," he said, with a hiss in his voice, "keep away from the Russians. God has cursed them! If you see that man again..."

Mariora went pale; she passed her hand vaguely over her forehead, and murmured, as if she were talking to herself: "That man! That's true... I'd forgotten him! But *he* won't forget me! He'll come back! He said that he would come back! Oh, my God! And you're going away. Mitica's going away, everyone's going... but *where* is everyone going?"

Light was probably dawning in her deceived mind–the cruel truth had probably been revealed to her in its entirety–when a cry of horror escaped her lips. Her wide open eyes were staring at a fixed point within the crowd, towards which she extended her arm.

"The man!" she cried. "The man–there he is!"

"Where?" said Ioan, attempting to clear a path through the throng.

"There! I can't see him any longer. Oh there, to the right, next to Relia Comanescu. He's mounted on his chestnut horse. Domna Rosanda's talking to him–he's smiling. Do you see him? Why is Relia dressed up like a *dorobantz*?"

Ioan did not reply. He had just recognized his adversary of the sunken path.

Liatoukine was here, insolent, fêted, surrounded by his friends. Domna Epistimia was offering him her hand.

66

Androcles Comanescu adopted a humble attitude in his presence. The noblewomen favored him with their softest smiles and their most ceremonious greetings.

"It's him!" murmured Ioan, though gritted teeth. "It's him! And I can't sink a dagger into his cowardly breast! I have to kill that man, though–I've sworn to do it! His name–who will tell me his name?"

But none of the common people knew the name of the foreign Colonel.

"When he passes close to me," Mariora sighed, near to fainting, "I go cold."

Mitica and Zamfira drew nearer. "Look, Zamfira," said Ioan, seizing the gypsy by the arm. "Look! That's the man who dared to insult the wife of Ioan Isacescu, the one who... the one against whom you must arm yourself and defend her. Do you understand?"

Zamfira crossed herself rapidly. "They say he's a vampire!" she said.

Mitica was silent. Ioan's simple words were translated, for him, into bitter reproaches, covering his forehead with a blush that he tried to hide beneath his military cap.

The Comanescus' calèche and Liatoukine's chestnut horse had disappeared in whirlwinds of dust in the direction of Bucharest. The four young people had arrived at the second roundabout on the Chaussée. It was nearly 7 p.m.; the air was warm and humid, and light grey clouds were missing in the north, which would hasten the dusk. Ioan saw them and stopped.

"We'll have to part here," he said, in a definite tone.

"Oh, no, Ionitza!" cried Mariora, dissolving into tears. "I don't want to leave you. I'll go with you as far as the station. I'll..."

67

"It's a long way to the Philarete Station, my poor love," he said, very gently, caressing the tearful Mariora's blonde hair. "The train leaves at 8 p.m.–see how the other *dorobantzi* are hurrying!"

Mariora tried to insist.

"Besides," he went on, more severely, "it's getting late, and even if you both walk quickly, you won't get home before it's completely dark."

"Ioan's right," Zamfira put in. "They have to leave us." Her eyes sought Mitica's.

The latter seemed prodigiously embarrassed; he was rooted to the spot, tugging at the feather in his cap as if to detach it. All of a sudden, he pulled himself together. "Zamfira! Zamfira!" he cried, hurling himself upon her. Placing his head on the gypsy's shoulder, he burst into tears.

Mariora, who had never seen her brother weep, stood there bewildered, not knowing what to think. "What's the matter?" she exclaimed. Then the contagion of the example took hold of her, and she started crying too.

Ioan ran from one to the other, rallying Miteca's courage, addressing words of consolation to Zamfira, and–most of all–making every effort to calm Mariora, who was crying even harder, although she was ignorant of the dangers her fiancé would be running, and had no reason to do so.

Besides, Ioan seemed more irritated than emotional. "It's getting late!" he repeated, incessantly. "We have to go!"

Finally, they all resigned themselves to following his advice. A kiss, a squeeze of the hand, a few words murmured in the ear, a lot of tears–and it was all over.

Mitica, sensing that emotion was getting the better of him, heroically followed in Ioan's footsteps.

The latter lingered beside Mariora. "Walk very quickly," he said to her, with a singular agitation. "Follow the main road, avoid the sunken paths and don't leave Zamfira's side. Do you understand? Don't leave Zamfira's side!" He emphasized the repeated words.

"I'll do as you say, Ionitza. Goodbye–come back soon, and don't forget me!"

"*Adio!*" cried the *dorobantz*, one last time–and the two soldiers went on their way towards the city, while all the Rumanian expressions reserved for such occasions resounded behind them: *La revedere! Cale bunà! Remaì sènàtos!* [23]

"He's gone!" said Mariora, when the crowd had swallowed up the two friends' white uniforms. "I've never seen Ionitza going away! How sad departures are!" A vague astonishment distressed her features. "Gone, gone!" she repeated. Her eyes could not tear themselves away from the spot where she had seen Ioan Isacescu vanish. "Come on, Zamfira, let's go," she sighed. "We've no more business here!"

The gypsy, however–who also had a heart, although Mariora seemed to have no suspicion of it–was lost in thought and did not reply.

"Well, what is it now?" said Mariora, acrimoniously. "Come back down to Earth, my beauty; think about the cheeses that are waiting for you, and the clouds that Ioan pointed out to you."

Zamfira's sky was so very dark, alas! She turned her eyes, which were full of dolorous surprise, upon Mariora. The latter, who presumably wanted to be forgiven for her ungracious manner, put her arm around the gypsy's waist, and they went back along the Chaussée in silence.

Zamfira was dark, Mariora was fair; Mariora knew that Zamfira served her as a contrasting foil, and she collected the flattering remarks of the handsome gentlemen whose paths they crossed with a secret pride.

Baba Sophia was an incorruptible guardian who did not permit anyone to play with fire; she only had to catch sight of a young boyar's moustache to start marching at a military pace, and Mariora had to follow suit whether she liked it or not. When her aged relative's skirts were not brushing hers, though, Mariora would take her revenge and would prick up her ears to listen— and a well brought-up girl, who appears not to understand anything, can still hear! When she compared the laudatory words of these brilliant unknowns to the slightly laconic severity of her future spouse, the comparison was not entirely to the latter's advantage.

The Chaussée, its noise and its strollers, no longer existed for poor Zamfira, whose excited imagination was evoking the most frightful scenes. There were terrible battlefields covered in corpses; there were towns in flames, their entire populations massacred. She heard the roar of cannon, the galloping of horses—and she thought she could make out Mitica's voice, rising above the imaginary racket, calling to her. She wanted to run to his aid, but Mariora's arm, which was holding hers, suddenly brought her back to a less cruel reality.

"My God, Zamfira!" her companion said, in a tone of lamentation. "It's ridiculous to run like this! When you're on your own, you don't walk so quickly that officers can't follow you!"

Zamfira slowed down, but she remained silent with regard to the unjust reproach, which was no kinder by virtue of coming from the mouth of Mariora Slobozianu.

Five minutes later: "My God, Zamfira! You're doing it on purpose. We'll never get out of the woods before nightfall. If you don't hurry up, I'll go back alone and Ioan will say that I was right!"

Zamfira bit her lip; her reserves of patience were exhausted.

A certain angry glance, which Mariora noticed, told her that a third observation of the same sort would probably be less well-received–but an evil genius seemed to have taken upon itself to counsel the priest's daughter that evening. She told herself that if Zamfira was angry, it was cause for rejoicing. While these ugly thoughts were circulating in her pretty head, she and her friend–or, rather, her victim–arrived at the entrance to the Baniassa woods. At the same moment, a group of young women irrupted into the principal thoroughfare; they let out cries of joy on seeing Zamfira and Mariora–to whom the unexpected encounter seemed extremely unwelcome.

"Hey, Zamfiritza! Hey, Mariora!" cried Ralitza, the brunette we have already met. "We're going back through Baniassa–are you coming with us?"

"I can't stand that little Ralitza!" Mariora muttered between her teeth. "She puts on airs, although she only has sandals on her feet." Zamfira was just about to accept the brunette's proposition when Mariora said, impertinently: "Speak for yourself if you wish, Zamfira, but I warn you that I won't accompany you where you want to go."

"But Ioan..." the Bohemian objected, timidly.

"Ioan couldn't foresee everything! You're free, and so am I. I know a pretty path that will spare me the tedium of keeping company with silly girls of your sort."

A German author of the 17th century said, in speaking of Rumanian women: "They are not, in truth, very good, but they are strong-minded, thinking much and saying little." The observation is quite just, save for the second point about saying little. That must have changed over time.

The young women knew that they would ruin everything by getting angry, but they lashed out with tongues, to such good effect that Mariora would have given her necklace of *rubias* [24] to take back her words.

"Oh! So the society of peasants like us doesn't suit you any more, my girl?" cried Katinka. "Someone must have made you a Princess."

"You're in a great hurry to be on your own! Ioan Isacescu hasn't left Bucharest yet, and you're already thinking of replacing him."

"It's done!" Ralitza put in. "Tell us, then, my beloved Mariora—what's you're new gentleman called? Konstantin? Nicolas? What?"

"Is he a handsome boyar, darling? A handsome boyar with pockets full of *galbeni* [25] and a mouth full of lies?"

"I'll bet he's an officer," said Florica.

"A Russian officer, hey, girl? One of those who talks *lubliubliubli*?"

"That's worth more than a simple soldier who's only got the uniform on his back and the love in his heart!"

"Aha!" said Ralitza, making a rapid movement to seize the hand that Mariora was hiding under her apron. "He's generous, your officer!"

Ioan's ring was revealed to all eyes, and was soon being passed from hand to hand, despite Zamfira's pleading and Mariora's invective. Scarlet with anger, Mariora tapped her dainty foot on the round and snatched the ring from the fingers of her jeering companions. "Give it to me!" she cried. "It was Ioan who gave it to me!"

The gleam of the copper and the delicacy of the engraving misled the young women as to the actual value of the metal.

"Ioan! Ioan!" they said, shaking their heads incredulously. "No peasant like your Ioan could have made you a gift of a ring that must have cost more than a hundred *leï*."[26] A hundred *leï* is the estimated cost of any glittering or unfamiliar object among Rumanian village women.

"Zamfira! Zamfira! Tell them that it was him who gave it to me!" cried the exasperated Mariora.

Zamfira's testimony carried more weight than her own, and she went on, indignantly: "Oh! You put less credence in my word than that of a gypsy! I know that you hate me–I know that you're jealous of me because my Ionitza..."

A burst of laughter, emitted with astonishing unanimity, drowned out poor Mariora's irritated voice.

"Your Ionitza! Your Ionitza! A fine bird, truly, for making us jealous!"

"Three hectares of land where wheat won't grow because the soil's too damp!"

"A hut whose roof lets the rain in, because Old Mani's too mean to have it repaired!"

"A rickety table, three chairs and two threadbare rugs for furniture, and what crockery! Great God!"

A smile brightened Mariora's features. "Ioan Isa-cescu isn't as poor as you think," she said, with dignity, "for I own nothing that doesn't belong to him."

She was truly beautiful when she spoke thus, and that unexpected reply appeared to have put a cap on the caustic verve of the disconcerted young Walachians, when little Ralitza, a true demon in petticoats, struck an ingenuous pose, biting the end of her thumb. "On that account, Zamfira isn't any poorer!"

A vivid blush covered the Bohemian's cheeks. She sensed that Ralitza's words were the first lightning-stroke of a storm that was about to descend upon her head.

Mariora went pale. "Zamfira!" she said, in a taut voice. "Zamfira! Ah, while the slightest breath of life animates Mariora Slobozianu, Mitica will never be the husband of Zamfira Mozaïs!" Taking a step towards the gypsy, she added: "You intend to be mistress of the Slo-bozianu household, do you? You want to have your own land! Tell us, then, what became of your sister Aleca?"

"Ale...Aleca?"

"Ah! You no longer remember Aleca, who was taken from behind by a Magyar magnate after he had espoused her, as one espouses the daughters of your race?"

"Aleca is dead!" said Zamfira in a dull voice, "and my father forgave her."

"And your brother, the renegade, who used to watch our flocks and now sells silks in Smyrna; your brother who named himself Serban and called himself a *Yezidee*;[27] your brother, who was born a Christian and is now no more than a pagan dog... if he isn't already dead and damned."

All that was true, alas; Zamfira could raise no objection, and large tears formed in her eyes.

"Mariora!" she begged.

Mariora was inflexible. "And your mother," she went on, spitefully. "That Nadejda, whom anyone could see dance for fifty *bani*." [28]

"My mother!" cried Zamfira, trembling with indignation.

Mariora fell silent momentarily. Then, with an attitude of inimitable disdain, she turned on her heel and said: "You, become Mitica's wife, when your own father probably doesn't know who you are!"

A general "Ooh!" of disapproval greeted these injurious words. If Zamfira had not held them back, the young women–who were by no means reluctant to take Mademoiselle Slobozianu down a peg–would have proved to the latter that their hands were not as light as their tongues.

"Little coward that you are!"

"It's a good job your brother isn't here to give you an answer!"

"An answer–along with another thing you deserve."

These epigrams were confused, like rifle-shots fired at a distance. Mariora went red and pale by turns. "Goodbye!" she said, in a changed voice. "We'll meet again!" And she went with a determined stride towards a copse that stood on left-hand side of the road.

"We'll meet again! That's what the city gentlemen say when they want to play with pistols after a drinking-session," said Katinka.

"Choose your weapons!" said Florica, putting her hand on her hip.

"Choose your time!" Ralitza continued, throwing back her head in such a fine parody of a braggart that the entire company sent a loud outburst of laughter echoing through the forest.

"Mariora!" cried Zamfira. "I don't want you to, but stay with us, in Ioan's name—or let me come with you!"

"She doesn't give a damn about Ioan Isacescu!" said Katinka, clicking her fingers above her head.

Mariora disdained to reply and plunged further into the bushes. Clematis and honeysuckle had invaded the place and were climbing the trunks of old beech trees. Mariora had difficulty making headway through the hectic confusion of the creepers. With her hands extended in front of her, she forced aside the rebellious branches, which sprang back to caress her face. She wanted to get as far away as possible from Ralitza and Zamfira, and the continual tickling of the foliage drew murmurs of impatience from her. Finally, the laughter faded into the distance, and the gypsy's plaintive voice, intermittently calling "Mariora! Mariora!" became less and less distinct.

Mariora was alone—alone in the Baniassa Woods at 8:30 p.m.–long after sunset!

The first thing that she did was to study the sky. A light southerly breeze had dissipated the grey clouds that were worth as much as a tart reprimand from Zamfira. Mariora seemed satisfied by the results of her observation; she redirected her gaze from the sky to the ground: thickets everywhere, save for a scarcely-perceptible path between oaks that had seen Michael the Brave [29] pass by.

"Finally!" she sighed.

That "finally" signified that she was very glad to be rid of the company, all the more so because it had not been easy for her to get away.

"The Sun set some time ago," she said to herself, "but the Moon's about to rise, and will light my way.

What pretty flowers! Nine o'clock hasn't sounded yet; I have time to gather a bouquet." And she set about plucking may-blossoms pitilessly, taking them somewhat randomly from the left and the right. She stopped occasionally and shook her head, as if to chase away an unwelcome thought; then she resumed her task with a kind of fervor. One might have supposed that she wanted to bring down on the innocent clematis the residue of her wrath, which she had not been able to pour upon the head of the Bohemian girl. The flowers that she had picked, unselectively, piled up in her apron.

Meanwhile, darkness was falling rapidly beneath the thick vault of the forest.

Like children, madmen and poets, Mariora had a habit of thinking aloud–a bad habit to nurture! She raised her head, and said, in a mildly commanding tone: "Where's that Moon that I'm counting on, then?"

With the good will that denotes the finest character, the Moon, thus summoned, hastened to display its plump red face within the dark blue of the sky.

"Ah!" said Mariora, who seemed to find it entirely appropriate to be immediately obeyed, even by the moon. "It's pretty, the Moon! Prettier than the Sun!" Then she added, by way of qualification: "Except that it never ripens the maize."

A ray of the moonlight that was powerless to gild the corn slid through the branches to strike Ioan's ring. Mariora studied it, admired it, turned it around in every direction–without, however, the ring recalling anything of the person who had given it to her.

Suddenly, she shivered; a familiar noise sounded close by. "Cuckoo! Cuckoo!" sang the bird.

She stood still, with one finger lifted and her mouth half-open.

"To the right? To the left?" she murmured.

"Cuckoo!" the bird repeated.

"To the left!" she cried. "An evil omen!"

She made the sign of the cross three times, in the Oriental fashion. Having perceived the ill-met bird perched on top of a wild cherry-tree, she picked up a little pebble, which she threw at the bird. It flew away, still towards the left, sounding its pitiful "Cuckoo!"

"Accursed creature!" said Mariora, letting her disconcerted gaze wander around her. Her eyes encountered the results of the pillage she had undertaken.

"That's no bouquet!" she said, woefully.

She let go of the corner of her apron, and the poor flowers went rolling at her feet.

"They were ugly!" she said, to console herself. Seized by a sudden resolution, she took a hundred paces in the direction of the village. But the young woman's courage diminished in inverse proportion to the deepening gloom. She began to find the Baniassa Woods much less pretty, and darted furtive glances at the bushes; but as she was afraid of nourishing her vague terrors by confessing them to herself, she attempted to drive them away by doing what the bravest folk do when they feel ill-at-ease: she began singing at the top of her voice.

Instinctively, she chose words full of pride and temerity; she boldly intoned the proud response of the architect Manoli in the popular ballad of *The Monastery of Argis*: [30]

"*There is nothing here on Earth*

"*To match our ten master masons*;

"*We'll build the most beautiful monastery*,

"*A monument to glory...*"

Her voice faded away. "I'm cold!" she said. Indeed, the temperature was descending towards that degree of coolness which ordinarily succeeds the intense heat of the day in Rumania, and which occasions the interminable fevers that have become a sort of national malady. But it was not the fever that was making Mariora shiver, and she launched into a long monologue, which a slightly less extravagant way of behaving would surely have spared her.

"Where are they now? Zamfira is wicked! Perhaps I did the wrong thing in not staying with them. I don't want her to marry Mitica, though! Yes, but I might perhaps have been too...too hard on her. I should have been able to make her understand with more tact. After all, it's not her fault that she loves Mitica! Love...that has come to me, of its own accord! Yes, but she has to avoid Mitica, and not reply to him if he speaks to her..."

"Will you go that far?" her conscience said to her.

A gust of wind set the leaves trembling agitatedly. Mariora went pale, and cocked her ear.

"I was wrong, definitely," she went on, after assuring herself that it was nothing. "It isn't Zamfira, it's me who has been wicked! It's no more her fault that Aleca let herself be carried away than it is that Serban became a Muslim or her mother danced for 50 *bani*! And me, in the presence of all her friends, I reminded her of it. Oh, I'm a miserable wretch!"

"Wretch," repeated the echoes.

"Poor Zamfira! She cried! But where can they be? I've been walking too–perhaps they're still not very far away. I'm very cold! It's so dark here! If I call out to them..."

She called out "Zamfira!" Then she waited.

"Zamfira!" replied the echoes, lugubriously.

Her own voice, coming back to her in modified form, chilled the blood in her veins.

"Zamfira!" she repeated, more feebly. "I won't do it again!"

"Zamfira! Again!" moaned the echoes.

"Oh!" said Mariora. "I'm afraid!"

Overwhelmed by discouragement, she sat down on the moist grass, put her head in her hands and began to weep. She had done it, alas! Night was closing in, and the wind was whistling in her untidy hair, to which leaf-debris was clinging. She wept like that for a long time, until she heard a sudden noise behind her, which made her get up. Making a whispered vow to light two fresh wax candles to the Virgin if she came back home safe and sound, she attempted to make her way back to the main road.

The main road was to her right, but the unfortunate girl was so troubled that she searched vainly to her left. She realized that she was completely disorientated, and began running straight ahead, no longer thinking of anything except finding the forest's edge. She was so sensitive to pain that pricking herself with her needle made her cry, but she did not feel the prickly holly-leaves that scored her hands and face–and when the moon, whose light was still her only guide, disappeared into the clouds, her ears perceived, along with the sinister *whee* of the wind, the beating of her own pulse.

Darkness and the unknown enveloped Mariora on all sides.

"Mitica! Ioan!" she cried–and terror lent a tone of profound desperation to the voice of the poor stray. But her brother and her fiancé were far away; they could not hear her.

She continued on her way in darkness, tripping on pebbles and bumping into tree-trunks. Will-o'-the-wisps emerged periodically from the marshy ground, their little blue flames seeming to wag accusatory fingers at the poor frightened girl.

*For being disobedient!* whistled the wind. *For being disobedient!*

Then, all the superstitions and legendary tales told by firelight came back into her mind. She gathered her exhausted strength.

"*Tata*! *Muma*!" [31] she called, hugging herself. But her father and mother were dead and unable to reply.

Mariora fainted.

When she recovered her senses, the Moon was shining with all its brilliance—but Mariora released a terrible cry and shut her eyes again.

Standing between her and the Moon was the spectral form of Boris Liatoukine!

*VI. "Mademoiselle Aurélie"*

Nicopolis [32] had just fallen under Russian domination, and a battalion of *dorobantzi* had been set to guard the western side of the town. *Bashi-bazouks* [33] had been seen prowling in the vicinity; there was fear of a nocturnal raid, and the soldiers had received orders to keep their eyes peeled and maintain complete silence. All the fires were put out; only one of the windows in the large white house that served as a temporary residence for the Rumanian commander, Colonel Leganescu, was illuminated by a feeble glow. Most of the soldiers were patrolling, weapons in hand; the rest were squatting on ground already strewn with shell-craters, testimony to the siege that the town had recently endured. Among the latter were the two friends from Baniassa.

"Two months gone by!" said Ioan Isacescu, shaking his head, "and no reply!"

"Bah!" said Mitica Slobozianu, who always found an explanation for everything. "Does anyone here care about letters to poor devils who ought not to know how to read? Do you have any idea what happens to our unfortunate scrawls? The Russians use them for lighting their cigars."

"Impossible!"

"When we took that infernal bastion over there... Lord Above, that was hot! I shudder to think about it..."

"Well," said Ioan, "What do you mean?"

"What I said," said Mitica, clicking his tongue. "Hidden behind a wall, General K*** was sitting up with a cigarette in his mouth, while all of that was raining down on us. He asked Captain Xenianine, in a perfectly natural tone, for a match. A match! He might as well have asked for a fresh egg! The captain took a tinder-box from his pocket and a dirty piece of paper, folded like a letter. 'Are you sacrificing a *billet doux* for me, Captain?' the fat clown [34] said, simpering. 'Not one of mine, incoming or outgoing,' Xenianine said, unfolding the letter. '*Iubita mia,*' [35] he spelled out, with some difficulty. 'That's Rumanian, I suppose?' He proceeded to roll up the paper quite calmly, lit it and presented it to the general. *Iubita mia*! A love-letter! Perhaps it was one of mine–I always start off like that."

"Might she be ill?" Ioan suggested.

"Bah! Don't waste time constructing futile hypotheses. They don't send the letters we write; why should they pass on the ones addressed to us?"

"Hey, comrades!" Scarlatos Romanescu called out to them. "They reckon we'll see *bashi-bazouks* tonight."

"Proudly armed with their *yataghans*!"

"They can decapitate a man! Look at this!" He bared his arm, which bore a wound more than eight inches long. "But they'll pay me back, the bastards!"

At that moment, the illuminated window opened.

"Send Lieutenant Zaharios to me!" called Colonel Leganescu.

"Lieutenant Zaharios can't walk, Colonel."

"What? Is he...?"

"He'll walk if you order him to, Colonel–but it won't be very straight."

"He's still drunk?"

"Two days straight, Colonel–and he's gone back for more."

Leganescu let out an expression that was more energetic than decorous. "I need a secretary, though," he murmured. He seemed to be examining the faces of the *dorobantzi* beneath his windows, one by one. "Isacescu!" he said, suddenly. "Come in here–we've go work to do."

"Lucky swine!" cried a chorus of soldiers when the door had closed behind their comrade. "He won't have to deal with the *bashi-bazouks*!"

A tawdry tallow candle stuck in a bottle spread its uncertain light through a large room, in the middle of which stood a table loaded with papers.

"Sit down, my lad," said Leganescu to his improvised secretary, "And let's get on with it!"

Ioan obeyed.

"To Brigadier-General Lupu..." the Colonel dictated.

For more than an hour, nothing was heard but the noise of the pen scratching the paper and the distant calls of the advance sentinels. Eventually, though, there was some animation outside. A horse dripping with sweat arrived at the threshold of the residence. Almost at the same moment, the door of the room opened, and a Cossack bearing an envelope sealed with the Imperial arms came in, with no more ceremony than if he were entering his guard-room.

Leganescu, who was somewhat resentful of the cavalier manners that the Russians had adopted, raised his head. "What is it?" he said, in Russian, in a distinctly churlish tone.

The Cossack bowed awkwardly. "It's a message from His Royal Highness Archduke Nicolas, addressed to Prince Boris Liatoukine."

"Prince Liatoukine isn't here. Go on, Isacescu! 'We are awaiting the fourth army corps, which...' "

"His Highness said that it's urgent," insisted the Cossack, "and ordered me to return immediately, without even entering Nicopolis. Can't someone carry...?"

Leganescu cut him of by rapping on the table with his snuff-box. "I have no *calaretzi* [36] here," he said. "They're all in the town." In Rumanian, he muttered: "How tedious he and his Archduke are!" He glanced sideways at his cherished heap of paper. "Isacescu, my friend, we've almost finished. Do you have any idea how to ride?"

Isacescu smiled. "You're forgetting, Colonel, that we Rumanians only quit the cradle for the saddle," he said.

"That's true!" Leganescu said. "Would you like to take care of this?" He threw the Imperial letter, with rather scant respect. "You'll find Prince Liatoukine over to the south–you'll have to ask, but someone will point you in the right direction. Hold on! You can use my own horse–take care of it, it's a thoroughbred!"

Ioan was eager to undertake the mission; the name of Liatoukine did not strike any chord within him. When he reappeared amid his brothers-in-arms, proudly perched on the Colonel's white horse, there was general astonishment.

"Since when did you join the cavalry?" several voices cried.

"Since five minutes ago." He gave them a brief explanation of his sudden promotion.

"Damn!" said Mitica. "You have all the luck! A little while ago, a secretary–now, an Imperial courier. You have your officer's diploma in your pocket, my dear chap!"

"I'd rather have a letter from Mariora!" he said, smiling, and he spurred his horse towards open country.

Meanwhile, on the far side of the town, four officers were walking in the moonlight. Three of them appeared to be in that state of merriment which ordinarily follows a copious meal lavishly washed down with fine wines. They were weaving from side to side, staggering somewhat, apparently aimlessly, when they saw a shadow coming towards them whose gait must have been familiar, for they aimed towards it and hailed it in these terms: "Hey! Yuri Mikailovich! Where are you going, all alone like that?"

"Nowhere, alas!" sighed Yuri Levine. "What about you?"

"Us?" said Bogomil, pursing his lips. "We're bored, and are in search of diversion."

"A rare commodity in these parts!" added Stenka.

"We're looking for a Rumanian," boomed Liatoukine's baritone voice. "A little Rumanian... to make him dance."

"That's a stroke of luck!" said Levine. Come this way. Over here, behind this hillock, there's one of our allies' sentinels–and you couldn't have chosen a better one, truly."

As if to confirm Yuri's words, an almost-feminine voice was heard sounding the challenge:

"*Cine e acolo?*" [37]

"*Prieteni!*" [38] called Liatoukine–and they went forward.

"Right!" said Bogomil, nudging his companions with his elbow. "I recognize the voice of the silliest and richest boy in Bucharest."

"What! Is that you, Comanescu?" cried Igor, feigning surprise. "Have they pushed irreverence to the point of giving you sentry-duty, like any common-or-garden plebeian?"

"Yao!" yawned young Relia, in an eloquently plaintive manner.

"Well, we'll relieve the sentinel," said Liatoukine, briefly.

"Impossible! I'm here by order of Colonel Leganescu."

Liatoukine was unwilling to allow the acknowledgement, at least in his presence, of any authority but his own. Relia's observation offended him, and he filed it away in a corner of his memory.

"And we're relieving you by order of Leganescu," Sokolich hastened to say.

"Ah, so much the better!" cried he young aristocrat, with an outburst of childish joy. Then, quite seriously, he went on: "Where, then, is my replacement?"

"Here," said Liatoukine, shoving Yuri Levine by the shoulders. The latter pulled a frightful face, accompanied a dull groan–but a glance from the Colonel reminded him that one did not trifle with the desires of Captain Vampire without severe consequences. He began standing guard without saying a word, while privately cursing the ridiculous whim of his superior officer, which was going to cost him six hours of additional duty.

Bogomil and Igor had each taken Relia by one arm, although the latter seemed more sustainer than sustained. Liatoukine marched on ahead–he had the air of a man leading a flock of sheep–while Stenka formed the rearguard. In this formation, the four friends and the little Rumanian arrived without further interruption at Liatoukine's lodgings–which is to say, the house of the late Aga, which Boris had "repatriated."

In addition to sums derived from legal contributions, this functionary had received, while alive, revenues from a host of petty taxes, which he had instituted to his own profit. In his apartments, Oriental splendor mingled with European luxury; there were brocade divans and Venetian glasses everywhere. The whole place was only slightly damaged by bullets, which had, fortunately, spared the bottles of French and Spanish wines that the good Muslim–who had reputedly been extremely devout–had crammed into his cellars.

The Aga's wine-cellar was immediately put to pillage by the young madmen, who wanted to revive the suppers of the Hugues Hotel on a Sardanapalesque scale.[39] The startled appearance and gross *naïveté* of "Mademoiselle Aurélie," who had no inkling of the fate in store for him, drew tears of hilarity from the officers, and the impassive face of Liatoukine, presiding over the orgy, was reminiscent of the skeleton that the ancients exposed during their feasts in order that its empty orbits and rictus smile might remind the guests of the brevity of human life–except that the sight of Boris did not evoke any funereal notion in brains already disturbed by the onset of inebriation.

"And you studied at the Collège Mabille, didn't you?" Bogomil asked Relia, putting as much interest into his voice as he could.

"You're mistaken," said the young man, with a candid smile. "The Mabille isn't a college, it's a dance-hall. Actually, I was at the Lycée Louis-le-Grand..."

"That's right–Louis-le-Grand!" Bogomil said, unctuously. "That's what I meant to say."

"We went out every Sunday," Relia went on, seemingly disposed to tell the exciting tale of his experiences as a student. "We went as far as the Arc de Triomphe. We were very tired when we got back. It was very enjoyable."

Stenka raised his head. "Mademoiselle Aurélie" was still smiling, and speaking very seriously. "He's too stupid for words," Stenka murmured in Igor's ear. Then, addressing the schoolboy, he said, rudely: "Didn't your mother ever send you anything?"

Relia's face lit up. "Oh, yes! Pots of jam!" And the memory of these preserves absorbed his mind so completely that he did not see his comrades smile.

"I was talking about money," Stenka said, shrugging his shoulders, "not sweets."

"Money? Oh, we had no need of money at the school–they fed us, lodged us..."

"Fed! Lodged! Here's a boy who's easily contented," Igor muttered behind his moustache.

"But when I was at university..."

"How many mistresses did you have?" Liatoukine said, abruptly.

Relia jumped in his chair and reddened to his ears. "Oh!" he stammered. "I never..."

"Come, come!" said Bogomil. "No secrets among comrades. Was she beautiful, eh?"

Relia turned scarlet, and plunged his nose into his glass.

"Was she beautiful?" Tchestakoff repeated, in a thunderous voice that made the poor student quiver.

"Oh, yes!" he sighed, finally, without raising his eyes.

"And what was her name?" Igor continued, intent on analyzing this youthful romance.

Relia allowed the words to be drawn out, as it were, from between clenched teeth. "Athénaïs Beaubuisson,"[40] he articulated, in a whisper.

"Athénaïs!" cried Bogomil, in a piercing one. "That's a splendid name!"

"Athénaïs means..." the student began, thinking that an etymological definition might serve to deflect the course of a conversation that was subjecting his modesty to torture.

"We're not concerned with philology," Sokolich put in. "We're talking about love."

The terrible interrogation got under way again, and Relia decided to take the confessional route.

"How old was she?"

"About 30."

"Damn! She was ripe!" Bogomil exclaimed.

"Pardon?"

"And did you see her often," said Tchestakoff, who rarely had difficulty maintaining his *sang-froid*.

"Oh! Not as often as I would have liked–once a month, when I went to pay the rent. I'd rather have paid the rent every day!" cooed "Mademoiselle Aurélie" in his softest voice.

"Pay the...*what*?" said Bogomil, who did not understand.

"The rent," young Relia repeated, complacently. "She was my landlady–in the Boulevard Saint-Michel, No. 55."

A gesture from Liatoukine stopped a loud burst of laughter on their lips, which would have shaken the windows of the room. Igor swallowed two large glasses of *selbovitza* one after the other; Stenka pulled the tips of his moustache; Bogomil's face disappeared under the peak of his cap. A beatific smile brightened Relia's features as he shut his eyes, to improve the passage through his imagination of the majestic silhouette of Lady Athénaïs Beaubuisson.

Stenka was the first to control his suppressed hilarity. He bowed to Relia, and said: "Well, my boy, you're stronger than I am. When I was at Heidelberg, where I scribbled essays in philosophy before making notches in the skin of my peers, I never got as far as domesticating my landladies–although it's true that they were older than 30 and I never went to pay the rent."

"I drink to our friend's *amours*!" said Bogomil, raising his glass. "To Madame Athénaïs Beaubuisson!"

"Boulevard Saint-Michel," Igor continued.

"No. 55," added Boris, maintaining his invariable grimace of a smile.

The glasses suspended their ascendant movement at shoulder-level. The three officers' mouths remained open; it was the first time that a pleasantry of that sort had ever escaped Captain Vampire's thin lips.

Relia wriggled in his uniform; unable to do anything but respond in kind, he seized the bottle of *selbovitza* that he found in front of him, mechanically, and drank directly from it.

"By the way," said Igor, gently retrieving the bottle from Relia's hands, "how do you say 'I love you' in Rumanian?" He added, thinking of a stylish little girl:[41] "It's bound to cost me some day, if I don't know how."

"*Eu te, iubescu*," said Relia.

"*You tay, youbesk*!" repeated Igor, jaw-wrenchingly. "A beautiful language, but a bit hard!"

"Comanescu, my friend, it would be very obliging of you to sing us one of your country's sings–a *doïna*–so that we can judge the genius of the idiom," Bogomil said, assuming a wheedling manner.

Domna Rosanda's teachings had borne their fruit, however. "Oh," said "Mademoiselle Aurélie," with a disdainful pout, "*doïne* are what the peasants sing."

"It's unnecessary to sully your aristocratic throat with plebeian airs," said Sokolich, sententiously. "In any case, we're not that fond of songs, are we, Colonel?"

Liatoukine sketched out a negative gesture.

"Since you won't sing," Bogomil, making himself more and more persuasive, "the least you can do is dance for us."

"Me, dance!" said Relia, with an ingenuous laugh.

"Colonel Liatoukine has expressed his intention to write an opuscule [42] on the various Moldo-Walachian dances, and he's counting on you to initiate him into the mysteries of the *hora*, which you shall dance for us forthwith."

"I can't dance the *hora* all alone," poor Relia replied. "It's a round dance."

"Oh well, you have the *batuta*, the piper and God knows what! There's plenty of choice."

"The *batuta*! The piper!" cried "Mademoiselle Aurélie." "But they're drunkards' dances!"

"Why should hold that you back?" Bogomil riposted, filling Relia's glass to the brim.

"Let's go, Monsieur–the piper!" [43]

The little Rumanian turned to his interlocutor, intending to protest–but Captain Vampire's gaze froze the words on the student's livid lips.

"Do you know what this is?" said Sokolich, setting before the bewildered young boyar a long lash made of hardened and creased leather. "We call this plaything a knout." He added, in a detached manner: "We make use of it in caressing the epidermis of recalcitrant soldiers."

Reflexively, Relia passed his delicate fingers over the thick stock of the instrument.

"It strikes hard," Bogomil said, with conviction.

"Monsieur Comanescu," Captain Vampire's strident voice resumed, "I'm not accustomed to giving the same order twice, you know."

Relia went pale, and tears came into his eyes. "But, Colonel..." he ventured. The little Walachian's attitude was almost supplicatory; he was reminiscent of a lamb at the mercy of a pack of wolves. With smiles on their lips and their formidable knouts in their hands, the Russians surrounded their victim and only seemed to be waiting for a word from Liatoukine to make use of their weapons.

"Let's go, little one, jump to it!" said Bogomil, ostentatiously lifting his whip. But Relia did not budge, and slowly shook his head. The Slavic blood he had inherited from his mother had not entirely annihilated the passive courage that is one of the dominant traits of the Rumanian character.

"One, two, three...hop!" howled Sokolich. The thong of the knout was already brushing Relia's hair.

"No," he said, in a firm voice.

And the knout came down.

In response to that degrading contact, Relia leapt to the other side of the room, his fists clenching convulsively. His blue eyes–ordinarily so soft–flashed, and with an energy that his frail and sickly appearance would scarcely have suggested, he cried: "Cowards! Are you not ashamed to attack a child?"

The epithet "cowards," so justly applied, brought the fury of he Russians–already excited by successive draughts of alcohol–to the boil.

"Oh, you refuse to recognize the power of our will!" they shouted. "Well, we'll show you how heavy our Muscovite arms can be! As we crush you, so we shall one day annihilate your miserable country, and all the men of your execrable race, if they aren't prepared to meet our demands!"

Under the frenetic impulsion of the bandits, the knouts clove the air and traced blue lines across the unfortunate young man's limbs. He was unable to defend himself.

Liatoukine, who had not abandoned his habitual indifference, came towards the damnable group, and moderated their ardor with a gesture. "You're striking too hard, gentlemen," he said.

Liatoukine's words and attitude exasperated the poor Rumanian. "And it's you," he cried, "that my father welcomed into his home like a son! Oh, you're even viler than your hired assassins!"

Liatoukine's eyes sparkled. "Don't add insult to your other sins, Monsieur," he said, gratingly. "You might have the opportunity to repent of them."

Relia fell silent. His gaze was caught and held by an enormous mirror, broken in several places, which was facing him; his features suddenly expressed a sentiment that partook of both joy and sorrow.

"I may be small and weak," he said, in a voice tremulous with hope, "but I'm not so completely forgotten and abandoned that I can't find a friendly soul to pity me and a powerful arm to protect me! Help me, Isacescu, help me!"

*VII. O Frailty...!*


The hiss of the whips died away. An unknown man of taller stature and coarser features had just appeared next to the exhausted and bloodied Relia Comanescu. His left hand was crumpling a wad of papers, and his right hand was extended, in a gesture replete with nobility, between the young man and his executioners. The man was evidently strong, and conscious of his strength. Without taking stock of the influence to which they were obedient, the Russians recoiled from him like jackals before a lion.

Relia had recognized Ioan; Ioan had remembered Relia. Ioan had repaid the debt contracted by Mariora, and the boyar's lip brushed the peasant's tanned fingers.

The *dorobantz*'s extraordinarily calm gaze surveyed the entire company, to various degrees. Not a muscle quivered in his face; one might have thought that no hatred had ever subverted his soul–and yet, his enemy was in front of him, nonchalantly perched on a divan, within range of his dagger! Ioan could see his enemy, though.

"Which of you is Boris Liatoukine?" he asked, coolly.

"That's me," said Captain Vampire, sitting up straighter. Ironically, he added: "Is your memory so short that you can't recognize me?"

The Imperial missive slipped from the messenger's fingers.

"Oh, yes, I recognize you," he said, with a bitter smile. "A Rumanian's memory is trustworthy, as is his *khanjar*! [44] But I did not know the name of the monster who takes pride in insulting old men, beating children an violating women!"

"My boy," said Bogomil, slapping Ioan on the shoulder and causing him to take a step backwards to avoid contact with the drunkard, "you're not very polite, and you talk like my Archimandrite uncle. No more of your pious sermons, I beg you; it's not Lent any more and morality gets on my nerves!"

An irritated glance from Liatoukine imposed silence on Tchestakoff.

"Are you alluding to the Slobozianu woman?" Boris said, calmly, picking the Archduke's letter up with the point of his saber. He continued, addressing his companions in debauchery: "It's to do with Mariora, gentlemen."

"Mariora!" exclaimed Igor, smoothing his moustache. "I knew her–a lovely sprig of a girl!"

"I knew her too–*she* wasn't shy!" said Stenka, performing a pirouette.

Ioan thought that he was in the grip of a horrible nightmare. The name of Mariora, which he produced as if it were that of a goddess, tripped from the mouths of these libertines accompanied by epithets! So they knew Mariora! Where and when had they known her?

This flood of questions was rising to the dry lips of the *dorobantz* when Bogomil, sticking both hands in his pockets, advanced towards him again, studying him with an impertinent curiosity. "Is it you, my boy, who is engaged to marry Maruschinka?"

"It is me!" said Ioan indignantly, "and I forbid you..."

"Well, I congratulate you–sincerely, I congratulate you," Tchestakoff repeated, with a false bonhomie–and he turned his broad back to resume his place.

Igor got up in his turn, and said, with the disdain that stamps the least movement and most insignificant remark of a great lord, from the heights of his nobility: "It's a great honor for you!"

Stenka's word became much clearer.

Ioan's knees buckled; a red mist passed before his eyes. "You're lying!" he cried, crushing the officer's arm in his own despairing grip. "You're lying!"

Stenka calmly disengaged his arm and elevated his shoulders. "I'm lying?" he said. "Just ask Liatoukine."

"Tell me that he was lying, and I'll believe you," Ioan said, in a muffled voice.

Liatoukine slowly offered his right hand to the *dorobantz*. "Look!" he said.

Shining amid the opals, the emeralds and the diamonds was the humble ring of Byzantine copper that Ioan had given to his fiancée!

"That isn't Mariora's ring," he said. He remembered the last letter of the Greek inscription had borne a particular mark–a little cross that he had engraved there with his dagger. He examined the ring minutely, and let Boris's hand fall back. The little cross was there!

"Mariora!" he cried, in a heart-rending tone. He darted a mad glance at all the men surrounding him, and released a frightful burst of laughter. "Oh, Mariora!" he repeated. Reflexively, his hand sought that of Relia, to whom the sight of his great anguish seemed strange, since he was weeping like a child. He was no longer thinking of vengeance. Mariora was dead to him; henceforth, his life would be purposeless, loveless...

And around the desolate pair, the Russians sniggered.

The sound of raised voices had attracted a dozen Cossacks. Liatoukine pointed them towards the two Rumanians.

"Twenty-five lashes with the knout for the little one," he said. "Fifty for the big one."

The next day, there was a singular agitation in the Rumanian camp. The officers, who took great pains to disguise their anger, conversed in hushed voices, while the soldiers–less circumspect–muttered death-threats at the mere appearance of a Russian cap. The rumor was running around that a Russian Colonel had had two *dorobantzi* whipped.

"The truth can sometimes be unbelievable." This line of poetry is nowhere more applicable than in Russia.

A roll-call of the *dorobantzi* regiment was effected immediately; two men were absent! Colonel Leganescu, to whom the duty fell, organized a rigorous enquiry, whose results established that, in addition to the ignominious punishment they had suffered, the two soldiers were still subject to imprisonment, which would last until the superior authorities ordered the unfortunates to be set at liberty. The place of their incarceration could not be ascertained.

This serious incident had the effect of enlivening the animosity that the Rumanians had nurtured towards their allies since the beginning of the campaign. The grievances of the Moldo-Walachians were certainly serious; they had not been spared humiliations of any sort. The Russians' ill-will manifested itself on the least pretext, and questions of precedence were invariably resolved in their favor; they had given the nickname "tin soldiers" to those whose military valor would save them a month later!

Several Rumanian officers from the same regiment as the injured parties challenged Russian officers to duels, and the clashes of swords and pistols behind the fortifications lasted more than three days.

In a solemn meeting that took place in Leganescu's quarters, it was decided that a demand for reparation would be addressed to Archduke Nicolas. General Cerneanu attempted to obtain an audience. Leganescu composed the request with typical Rumanian brio, which is better suited to a dash of eloquence than a simple Colonel's report, and the secretary Zaharios, who had recovered the use of his legs, inscribed the names of Aurelio Comanescu and Ioan Isacescu in his finest handwriting.

Cerneanu, having received the letter granting him an audience, presented himself at the Russians' general headquarters, not without having made several cuts in Leganescu's manuscript. In various passages, the latter, attentive to legitimate indignation, had neglected the principles of courtly politeness that one must employ in addressing Archdukes.

The interview did not last long. From the moment that the Russians received a Rumanian officer, all ceremonial formulas were suppressed; a Cossack *shoved*–for want of a better word–Cerneanu into a low-ceilinged room, which served an antechamber, and after half an hour's wait, the General was introduced into the Archduke's apartment.

The Archduke's apartment bore a strong resemblance to those of the corrupt Aga of whom mention has been made. There were a great many *objets d'art*, and luxurious furnishings of exceedingly various provenance, assembled in haste. All these broken beautiful things gave such a strong impression of being elements of booty that the sight of them only gave rise to thoughts of sacked towns.

Not far from a table, on which were set a few pamphlets on strategy, the petty apparatus of a smoker and a glass of water, Nicolas Nicolaevich was lounging in an armchair that had belonged to an English businessman resident in Nicopolis. The Prince did not appear to be more than 45 years old; an expression of calm hauteur, which impressed all those who came in contact with him, was spread upon his features, which were much more regular than those of the Tsar and Archdukes Constantin and Michael. He was listening to the monotonous voice of a blond and rosy-cheeked aide-de-camp, who was reading an article from the *Golos*.[45] The reading did not seem to interest His Highness very greatly; he was yawning with Muscovite off-handedness.

"Enough, Xenianine, enough!" said the Prince, on perceiving the General's epaulettes. Xenianine fell silent and got up to leave; a sign from the Archduke immediately re-nailed him to his seat.

"What is it, Monsieur?" Nicolas said, raising his head slightly towards Cerneanu, in the dry tone he used to address everyone except his older brothers.

The General bowed, respectfully, but without any servility. His gesture displeased the Archduke, who thought the old man's dignified behavior irreverent.

Cerneanu explained, in a few words, the purpose hat had brought him to the Archduke's headquarters. The Prince interrupted him with a slight gesture of impatience.

"I know, I know, Monsieur," he said, putting out his hand. "Is that your report? Give it to me."

In the Russian army, the knout replaced or forestalled the reports that the Prince hated. The Archduke riffled through Leganescu's voluminous screed and his eyebrows slowly came together; he was annoyed.

"Well, Monsieur," he said, passing the report to Xenianine, "what is there to complain about? The two men are guilty. One, according to his own admission, abandoned the post that had been entrusted to him by one of your own officers. The other spoke words injurious to Prince Liatoukine–who, by only having a restricted number of strokes administered, has shown himself to be very lenient."

The Archduke imparted powerful shaking movements to the English businessman's armchair as the sentences fell from his lips like pebbles on a zinc plate–but the arguments that he thought worthy did not appear forceful to the Rumanian General, who resumed calmly: "I will point out to Your Highness that the sentinel Comanescu was relieved by Prince Liatoukine himself, and that Corporal Isacescu was forced to rescue his comrade from the ill-treatment to which Russian officers were subjecting him before the very eyes, and with the approval, of the aforesaid Prince Liatoukine."

Cerneanu's logic was a sovereign irritant. Nicolas Nicolaevich understood that he was dealing with someone cleverer than he, and that, if the discussion continued much longer, his adversary would undoubtedly win a victory. In order to avoid a conclusion insupportable by his personal vanity, His Highness took the course of raising the pitch of his voice and becoming violently angry.

"Those are details, Monsieur!" he cried. "Details that are of no importance to us! There was wrongdoing, as I hope you will certainly admit; in consequence, there must be punishment!"

The armchair creaked and water from the glass sprayed the wall–but archducal extravagance did not have the power to move Cerneanu, who went on calmly: "The dishonorable nature of the punishment, however..."

The Archduke leapt to his feet.

"This is a joke, Monsieur," he said, setting off to stride across the entire length of the room. "The dishonorable nature of the punishment!" he repeated, sarcastically. "Should your compatriots have been awarded the Cross of St George, perhaps?" he shouted, striking his spurs against the floor-tiles in his fury.

The General, who had not been invited to sit down, endured the Archduke's sarcasm with remarkable coolness. "Among my people," he said, gravely, "the officers have too much self-respect to venture to raise their hands against their inferiors."

Nicolas Nicolaevich sank back into his armchair with a burst of bitter laughter. "Among your people, Monsieur–your people! My opinion is that your people tend to forget what they are!"

The armchair swiveled around. In response to a gesture from the Archduke, who was disposed to light a cigar, Xenianine's nasal voice sounded again, in the midst of a profound silence, to observe in Russian that the enemy was attacking within the town.

Cerneanu sensed that he was reddening to the hairline under the insult inflicted upon him, and his hand, tremulous with indignation, let the velvet door-curtain fall behind him.

The entire Rumanian camp assembled in front of the old General. On seeing their faces, full of anxious impatience, Cerneanu shook his head sadly.

"Oh, men!" he said, with an accent whose bitterness was indescribable. "What are we doing on this side of the Danube?"

A fortnight after that characteristic scene, a company of Cossacks returned the two heroes of this deplorable adventure–which was on the point of causing an abrupt breach in the amicable relationship between Alexander II and Charles I–to their company.

Relia Comanescu, dazed and dejected, was slumped on his friend's arm. His badly-scarred wounds were causing him to suffer cruelly and he fainted in front of General Cerneanu, who was his cousin in the British sense–which is the same as the Rumanian sense.

Ioan Isacescu, on the other hand–whose robust constitution rendered him less sensitive to physical suffering–was marching proudly, with a smile that was almost joyful. A Cossack observed that he had taken his 50 strokes of the knout cheerfully. He seemed to have undergone a complete transformation; he had the inspired expression of a visionary or a martyr, and his eyes were, so to speak, fixed on something inside himself.

Mitica marched straight towards him, while he slid his fingers over the horny hilt of Old Mani's dagger. "For Liatoukine!" he said. Then, half-drawing the *khanjar* suspended from his belt, he murmured: "For Mariora!"

## VIII. Saint Alexander's Day

Eventually, time always soothes the sharp pains that translate into plaints and sobs, but mute pains are beyond its beneficent scope.

Ioan no longer mentioned Mariora's name.

The *dorobantzi* and the *caletzi* were encamped around Pleven. They met ambushes at every step and were perpetually involved in skirmishes, but these multiple dangers were no match for Ioan's ardent boldness. He took up the most perilous positions and often embarked on scouting missions behind the Turkish lines in the middle of the night, at the risk of being killed or taken prisoner.

His superiors held that courage in great esteem; it brought them valuable information about the lie of the land, the hazards of the terrain and the enemy positions; his peers compared him to Codrean,[46] and invariably spoke of him with admiration. Sometimes he came back from his solitary expeditions laughing silently, as had become his habit, his rifle reeking of burnt powder even though no Muslim had been seen in the vicinity.

"Isacescu knows well enough why he laughs!" the soldiers said, nodding their heads in a particular way.

He had a singular manner of fighting. In mid-battle, he would suddenly pause, his finger poised on the trigger of his rifle, his eyes fixed on some point on the horizon. The memory of Mariora would return to his heart; he saw her as a little girl, running through the maize with her blonde hair in disorder; he heard her voice, her infantile voice, saying "*Ionitza meù*" and he listened. Then the hammer would fall, with a dry click, and a man would fall in the distance. Russian or Turk? How could anyone tell?

His words were as bizarre as his actions. In one forward engagement, the barrel of his revolver ran into the breast of an Ottoman. "Why should I kill this man, who has never done me any harm?" he said, aloud–and, without even seeing the pitiful tears running down the poor Turk's cheeks, he lifted up his weapon, took aim, and fired–and a Cossack slid from his horse.

Isacescu burst out laughing.

"Ah, the hazards of battle! I *am* the hazards of battle!"

He ran around the battlefields without fear of *bashi-bazouks* and Cossack marauders, a muffled lantern in his hands, examining and handling every cadaver.

"What are you looking for, comrade?" someone said to him.

"I'm looking for someone I'd rather find standing up," he replied.

One day, in the heat of battle, he had an impulse to flee, to return to Rumania. He took a few steps backwards, then came back to face the Turkish gunfire. He captured one of their flags–but heroes who have 50 lashes on their record are given no medals.

General Cerneanu, to whom the Tsar had sent a prodigious number of Crosses of St George, regretted not having the power to award one to the brave *dorobantz*; by way of compensation, he gave him a handshake, less banal than the Muscovite decoration.

Mitica pounded his own cross repeatedly, and when it was no more than a slug of metal, he threw it in the river Vid, crying: "I don't want their filthy gold!"

Cerneanu saw the gesture and heard Miticas's exclamation, but he did nothing about it; soldiers and officers alike hated the Russians.

On the morning of September 11, the old General, who was the idol of the Rumanian army, brought his troops together and addressed this short speech to them:

"Men, there's a black dot yonder, hidden in the mist; it's called the Gravitza Redoubt. We have to take it. We'll have shellbursts above our heads, bayonets in front of us, powder beneath our feet–the redoubt is mined–and behind us, Archduke Nicolas. It seems that today is the Tsar's birthday. It's a matter of regaling His Majesty with a fine spectacle. I must see you all killed rather than retreat–that's the Imperial order. Believe your old friend–we're doomed! It's not pleasant to have to tell you that, but you've seen others do it and you'll die stoically in the breach, like the sons of Rumania that you are. Put your affairs in order immediately, and if you have any money, deposit it at headquarters; it'll be sent to your relatives. Can I count on you?"

"We'll follow you, General," the unanimous voices of the soldiers replied. On every face, though, the enthusiasm of the warrior was replaced by the bleak resignation of the condemned.

Relia, however, was devastated. He was fearful and timid, as the majority of children are whose mothers do not love them. Death terrified him, just as darkness did. His heart was tender, accessible to common sentiment; he had understood that devotion is a rare plant, which often grows better in plebeian hearts than in those the boyars call *well-born*. This poor, essentially inoffensive, creature felt that without Ioan Isacescu, he was nothing but a leaf thrown into the course of a torrent, and he had devoted to his savior a friendship and idolization that manifested themselves in complete submission and eternal protestations of childish affection.

"Brother!" he cried, hurling himself into Ioan's arms. "We'll be massacred."

"Yes," Ioan said, impassively.

"I have some poison. Do you want some? It'll be quick, and we'll suffer less."

"Yes."

Relia handed him a little packet full of white powder, which he had taken from his belt.

Ioan tipped it all out into a water-filled ditch.

"What! What are you doing?"

"My duty. It's our last day–let's not be cowards."

"Oh–but the Turks will do terrible things to us."

"No worse than others have done to us."

"I'm frightened, brother. You won't leave me, will you?"

Ioan remembered that those same words had once been spoken to him by Mariora. "No," he said.

Relia sighed. "Oh, you're lucky to have courage. I'm afraid of the crows, brother!"

"When the crows arrive, the pain is ended."

"I don't want to be buried here," the child groaned. "I want to go back to my own land–Rumanian ground! Who will take me back to Rumanian ground?"

"Me."

"You?" cried Relia, with an incredulous smile.

"If you die, I'll carry your body to headquarters, and you'll be able to sleep in your native soil."

"Oh, is that true, Ioan? You'll do that! And me–what shall I do for you, useless creature that I am?"

"When I'm dead, you'll take my large dagger with the horn handle, and you'll search out Liatoukine."

Cerneanu gave the order to sound the call to arms.

Mitica, who had been helping to carry the wounded into the wooden huts that served as temporary hospitals, buckled his belt hurriedly and seized his rifle. A feeble voice close at hand murmured the word "*Frate!*"–the Rumanian word for brother, so sweet to the heart of a Rumanian far from home. Very surprised to hear a Walachian word from the mouth of a Turkish soldier, Mitica drew nearer.

"Brother," the wounded man repeated, lifting himself painfully on to his elbow, "are you from the Rumanian land?" *The Rumanian land*, in the strict sense, is Walachia.

"I'm from Bucharest," Mitica replied.

A sudden joy illuminated the dying man's disfigured features. "From Bucharest?" Letting his head fall back on the cartridge-box that served him as a pillow, he sighed: "Bucharest is so magnificent!"

"I'm from the neighborhood of Baniassa."

"Baniassa! Do you know old Mozaïs, Aleca and Zamfira, then?"

"Do I know Zamfira?" Mitica exclaimed. "If I ever get back there, I'm going to marry Zamfira!"

The Muslim's dull eyes recovered a little of their sparkle. He studied Mitica attentively, saying: "I've never seen you before."

"That's not surprising, comrade!"

Blood was running freely from the dying man's breast; his fingers were designing vague symbols in the air. "Well," he said in a scarcely intelligible voice, "will you go to old Mozaïs...and...tell him...that..."

"Your name–quickly, what's your name?" Mitica said, insistently, feeling the unknown man's hand growing cold in his own.

"I'm... I'm..." His lips kept moving, but he could not articulate another syllable.

He died, taking his secret with him.

Mitica remained beside the body, pensively, for a few moments. He lowered the mysterious *Osmanli*'s eyelids and wrapped him in a dirty linen sheet; then, very thoughtful and annoyed with himself, he hastened to rejoin his regiment.


The *dorobantzi* set forth into the mud and the mist. The mud was thick, and made their march difficult; the fog was dense, and penetrated their clothing. Their mouths were shut. Their eyes were aflame. Did the Russian Emperor's dreams show him what was in those men's eyes?

Sometimes, a murmur ran through the ranks; a few ironic voices would cry "It's Saint Alexander's day!" and then everyone would fall silent.

They advanced in this manner for about an hour. Gravitza could not be far away; the noise of the cannonade was not so dull; the first projectiles were cleaving the damp-sodden air. The daylight was merely a grey twilight. The soldiers advanced at hazard.

Where was Gravitza? To the right or the left? No one knew.

"This is the beginning, men!" cried General Cerneanu. "Hold fast, and remember..."

"That it's Saint Alexander's Day?"

"No! That you're Rumanians!"

A violent fusillade burst forth; an atrocious clamor became audible.

"What's that, General?"

"A regiment dying."

"Where?"

"To the left, in the valley; follow me, men!"

Relia stuck fast to Ioan's side, mentally reciting the prayers that Domna Rosanda had taken the trouble to teach him.

"You're frightened, little one," said a Corporal with a scar on his forehead.

"I want to get out of here!" sobbed "Mademoiselle Aurélie," rolling his startled eyes.

"Well, we're getting out, my lad, sooner than we might wish!"

"Hurrah! The dead go quickly!" cried a Sublieutenant from Leipzig. "We're dead, or very nearly!"

"*Ajutatzi! Ajutatzi!*" [47] These despairing cries rising up from the valley reignited the Rumanians' anger.

"Throw away your rifle," Ioan said to the distraught Relia, "and give me your hand."

Relia obeyed mechanically.

Brave *dorobantzi*! They hurled themselves into the valley, more ardent than the *zmeï* of legend! The slopes were slippery, the men rolled over one another. It was raining lead. The incessant Turkish musket-fire tore frightful holes in their ranks. What did that matter? Comrades were in danger; they had to be saved, or, at least, one had to die with them! Smoke combined with the fog. Blood and mire mingled. Dead men–dead men everywhere! The valley slowly filled up. A bullet struck the regiment's ensign. "The standard!" cried a dying voice. "Protect the standard!"

Mitica took possession of it; whining bullets passed through the tricolored pleats of the flag.

"The Turks shall not have the standard," he said. The explosions succeeded one another more rapidly; little by little, the air was clearing.

"Well, men?" said a voice in the mist.

"Well, General, there's a trench... it's ours!"

"The nation shall know your names, my lads, and Europe shall know the nation's name!"

Relia did not have a single scratch. He was astonished to find himself alive. "Is it over now, Ioan?" he said, fearfully.

"Not yet. After the trench, the redoubt."

"Oh, my God! And...are there still Turks within it?"

"Of course! If there weren't, the redoubt would be taken!"

"Mademoiselle Aurélie" resumed trembling; Ioan drew him on.

The Rumanians scaled the opposite slope. They were no longer thinking about Saint Alexander's Day; they were thinking about the fatherland, positions to be taken–of all the ingredients of glory, in sum.

"Hey, Mitica Slobozianu! I've got a graze here that'll get me a Sublieutenant's epaulettes."

"The taking of Gravitza! What a great story to tell at parties, eh?"

"Unfortunately, no one will believe us–we've told too many lies!"

"Our scars will shut the mouths of the incredulous."

"When I become an officer, I'll marry a city girl."

He was not even to marry a peasant; a Muslim bullet put a permanent end to the young Walachian's proud ambitions.

They were truly splendid in an attack, these "tin soldiers"! How they climbed! And how they died, with smiles and jokes on their lips! They really were, as they said to another with legitimate vanity, *the Frenchmen of the Orient!* Within a quarter of an hour, the redoubt would surely be taken. The first rank had arrived at the top of the hill crowning the Turkish earthworks.

Suddenly, a cry–a howl of rage–emerged from thousands of throats, which struck the Tsar's ears from afar. The *dorobantzi* recoiled in consternation...

"Damnation!" cried General Cerneanu, in a voice that had nothing human in it. "There's a ravine between the redoubt and us!"

"I told you, General," Ioan said. "We'll cross the ravine."

"We'll cross the ravine," a powerful echo repeated.

At that same moment, a plaintive moan was heard from Ioan's side. Relia's grip relaxed.

"Ioan," he murmured. "The crows..." And he fell, as if struck by lightning, at his friend's feet.

Ioan remained motionless. His eyes went from the wounded man's face, already pale, to the silhouette of the redoubt, outlined in black against the brown. He hesitated between the duty that called him to his companions and the friendship that retained him at his adopted brother's side. A sigh from the unfortunate child sealed his decision. He loaded and fired his rifle one last time. While rapidly making the sign of the cross, he said: "My God help hem and pardon me!" Then he added: "I'll come back!"

He lifted Comanescu–who weighed hardly any more than Mariora–effortlessly. "Put your arm around my neck," he said to him.

But Relia did not put out his arm.

By clutching with one hand at tufts of grass and lump of rock, and digging his heels into the damp clay, Ioan managed to keep his balance, and regained the valley floor. Beneath a projecting block of granite, he perceived a few feet of ground carpeted with moss, which was scarcely dirtied; judging it to be a fairly safe shelter, he deposited his burden there.

There was not a drop of blood soiling Relia's white shirt; had it not been for the pink foam seeping from his lips, one would not have suspected that he was wounded.

Ioan parted the *dorobantz*'s clothing. The bullet had pierced the chest in the vicinity of the heart; the wound was slightly moist, but all the blood was in the pleural cavity.

Ioan shook his head. "A mortal wound that doesn't bleed!" he murmured.

Hastily, he improvised a dressing that he knew to be futile, and set about crawling between the corpses, carefully feeling the officers' belts. He soon came back with a flask half full of *selbovitza*. He unclenched Relia's teeth with the aid of his dagger, and introduced a drop of the beneficent liquor into his mouth.

The young man moved convulsively, and put a hand to his breast. An expression of indescribable terror overtook his features. "The crows!" he stammered, and fainted again.

"Let's go!" said Ioan to himself. "One Rumanian doesn't abandon another."

Loading his friend on to his strong shoulders, he began slowly climbing the other slope of the valley. The descent had not been easy, but the ascent was painful. Ioan was continually bumping into irregularities in the ground, and more often still into body-parts clinging to old tree-trunks. He provided a target for the Turkish carbines; one bullet went straight through his cap, from back to front, another through the sleeve of his uniform. The slightest false step might have sent the courageous Walachian tumbling in a fatal fall, but a mysterious power seemed to be protecting him. After half an hour of anguish and extraordinary effort, he reached the top of the slope.

When he saw that he was in open country, he felt that he was safe. Presenting the flask to the unconscious Relia's tight lips, he examined his friend's discolored features with fraternal affection.

"Poor boy!" he said. "Another ten minutes and he'll be finished." A tear, quickly wiped away, glistened in the soldier's eye. "He was good, but he wasn't brave," he added, as if to justify his moment of weakness.

A few horses–poor riderless beasts–were wandering in his vicinity. Murmuring the magic word *puiu*,[48] well-known to Rumanian cattle and horses, he went up to one of them, which seemed to him more vigorous than the rest, and capable of undertaking a long trek. The horse whinnied and offered itself to the caresses of a benevolent hand.

Then, lifting Relia in his arms as mothers do with little children, Ioan set his feet in the stirrups, and the horse set off like an arrow, carrying the two riders. The gallop was so rapid that the horse's shoes hardly seemed to touch the ground. The redoubt receded to the horizon, and Ioan soon perceived the outlying fires of the Russian encampment. He reined in his ardent mount in front of the door of a pretty cottage, which he took to be a hospital.

"Hey! Hey! What's this?" said the churlish voice of a Cossack.

Ioan spoke Russian well enough, having learned it in Nicopolis. "Open up–it's a wounded man."

"A Russian?"

"No, a Rumanian."

"We don't want any wounded men here–the Tsar's in the house."

"But you can surely see that he's dying."

"All the more reason! It's Saint Alexander's Day; the Tsar is here, as you've been told. We're not receiving dead men. Go away!"

"Where shall I go, then?"

"To your own lot. They're over there, mimicking our general headquarters as best they can. There's some sort of Colonel they call Leganescu."

In other circumstances, the Cossack's insolent words would have rebounded, metamorphosed into blows with the flat of a saber, upon his own barbarous spine.

"At least give me a cart," Ioan persisted.

"There are no carts here! Go away, as you've been told!"

And the Cossack slammed the door.

Ioan knew the Russian character well enough not to be astonished by these inhuman proceedings. He made a gesture of disgust, dug his spurs into the flanks of his horse, and the fantastic ride became even more so, by the uncertain light of the rising Moon, huge and pale in the mist.

The cool of the night and the repeated leaps of the chestnut horse, an impetuous emulator of Calul Vintesh,[49] were more successful than the *selbovitza* in reviving the spark of life that still animated Relia. He recognized Ioan, smiled, slid his fingers into the dorobantz's belt and closed his eyes again with a sigh.

*Poor Aurelio!* Ioan thought, pressing his friend to his bosom. *The empty space he leaves behind isn't very large in the hearts of his family! Who loved him? Whom has he loved? Me–and me alone! While he's dying here, his mother and sisters are running from ball to ball, listening to the ridiculous flatteries of the Russians who have killed him. His father doesn't even know what peo-*

115

*ple call him!* "He's a boyar! Ah, poor little boyar!" he cried, aloud, in a tone in which pity was laced with slight disdain. His face suddenly darkened; his gaze, which was almost hard, came to rest on Relia's feminine traits. "And in 50 years time, this child would have been my master!"

He lost himself in his reflections–and, while telling himself that a boyar was a very little thing, unworthy of being carried in the arms of a son of the people, and that men were all equal before God and circumstance, he arrived at the Rumanian headquarters. Relia did not seem to want him to dismount, though; his hand would not let go of Ioan's belt.

"We're among friends," Ioan said, taking his foot from the stirrup.

Relia did not reply, and continued to hold his companion back. Ioan then realized that he was dead.

At the sight of the corpse, Colonel Leganescu bared his head, with the respect Rumanians show to that which has been a man. "His name!" he asked, in a soft voice, as if he feared to trouble the dead man's sleep.

"Aurelio Comanescu, from Bucharest," Ioan replied.

"Cerneanu's cousin! The one who..."

Ioan interrupted him. "Yes," he said, and added, simply: "I'm the other."

Leganescu slapped his forehead. He drew the *dorobantz* nearer to the nightlight, which gave birth to more shadows than brightness in his tent. "That's right!" he said. "I remember you!" He paused, then resumed: "My boy, forgive me for the harm I did you, indirectly, by sending you to that incarnate Beelzebub."

"On the contrary, Colonel–I thank you."

Leaving Leganescu to his astonishment, Ioan departed, after depositing a last kiss on Relia's cold forehead. Then, as he had said he would do, he set off again for Gravitza.

The ravine had been crossed, but the redoubt had not been taken. "Curse it!" he cried.

The odor of blood and gunpowder caused him instantly to forget Relia, Mariora, perhaps even Liatoukine. He threw himself into the battle, thrusting with his saber, taking aim and firing, with a kind of desperation. He was terrible thus, and the Turkish corpses piled up around him.

He caught sight of Mitica's tall figure in the distance, defending the Rumanian eagle, removed from its staff, against a furious attack. That vision lasted two seconds before everything before his eyes became confused.

In spite of General Cerneanu's incontestable skill and the unbreakable courage of his soldiers, the Rumanians were visibly losing ground. Strategy could achieve nothing in the face of that thunderous artillery; it required men—men who would have formed a wall of flesh thick enough to impenetrable to bullets.

Cerneanu tore his hair and, while still exhorting what remained of his troops, he murmured: "We won't make it! We won't make it!"

"Hurrah!" a voice suddenly shouted, resounding like that of an angel of salvation in the besiegers' ears. "Colonel Boris Liatoukine's bringing us reinforcements!"

All eyes turned, and all hopes too, towards the Cossack regiment that was emerging from the mist like an army of phantoms in a dream—and while the Rumanians greeted the unexpected apparition with repeated cries of

*Traiéscà Russia!* [50] Ioan, suddenly reclaimed by the idea of vengeance, murmured: "Liatoukine! Before the present hour is over, my dagger will have seen the color of your blood!"

Despite the profound obscurity of that fatal night, in spite of the distance that still separated him from Liatoukine, he recognized his adversary easily by his tall stature and his strident voice, which rose above the various noises of battle like the blast of a clarion.

Ioan reloaded his revolver, even though he did not expect to make use of it. The accomplishment of what he considered an act of justice was solely reserved for Old Mani's knife. He loosened that terrible weapon–which was nothing but than a long *yataghan* snatched from the hand of a *bashi-bazouk*–in its leather scabbard.

Rumanians are as indifferent in religious matters as they are strong in superstition. Ioan signed himself more by habit than devotion. "Boris Liatoukine is dead," he said.

Clearing a path through the ranks of the *dorobantzi* and the Cossacks, stepping over the heaps of uniforms, beneath which a few items of bloody debris still stirred, he succeeded in reaching Captain Vampire.

"It's me!" he said, with a hateful stare that would have disconcerted a man less sure of himself than the Colonel.

The latter studied him coldly, apparently neither annoyed nor surprised. "I've been expecting you," he said, dismounting. In a casual manner that the fine gentlemen of Bucharest would have admired, he threw the bridle of his horse to an aide-de-camp.

"Leave us, Dmitri Nikitich," he said. He turned towards Ioan. "Come with me," he said. "This place is scarcely appropriate for conversation."

Ioan followed him, with his revolver in one hand and his dagger in the other. Contact with these weapons heated the Rumanian's feverish fingers, and the sharpened point of the *yataghan* caressed Liatoukine's clothing.

*There aren't two cowards here*, Ioan thought, recoiling slightly. *I don't want to stab him in the back!*

When there were no longer any but dead men around them to serve as witnesses, Liatoukine turned. "Well," he said, "what do you want with me?"

"What do I want?" Ioan cried, in a voice broken by sorrow and anger. "He asks what I want! Will you efface the brand from my father's forehead that your whip imprinted there? Can you render my honor intact, which you threw as a bone to the dogs who flatter your odious whims? Can you give me back my Mariora? Can you do that? If so, I'll forgive you."

"Cut it short!" said Liatoukine, nonchalantly brushing off the mud that stained his clothing.

"Mariora! All the gold in the world cannot repay me for my Mariora!"

"Pooh!" said the Russian, with a gesture of indifference. "If it's gold you want, you can have it." And he made the rubles in his belt clink.

This new insult changed Ioan's wrath into a furious madness. He leapt towards Liatoukine with a raucous cry. "I want the last drop of your blood, the last breath from your lips! I want your life!" he howled.

"My life?" repeated the impassive Prince. "That's easily said, my boy!"

"No more words, Boris Liatoukine! One of us will die, I swear! Defend yourself!"

Ioan applied the barrel of his revolver to Liatou-kine's breast. The latter shrugged his shoulders, an enigmatic smile playing upon his features.

An explosion resounded, the blade of the dagger glittered in the sinister rays of moonlight, and Captain Vampire, still smiling, collapsed without uttering a plaint or releasing a sigh.

The warm sensation of the blood that ran in rivulets over his hands only served to excite the Walachian's rage. The Byzantine ring caught his eye; it was very tight–Liatoukine had been wearing it for more than three months. Ioan, unable to remove it quickly enough from the dead man's finger, cut it away; he placed it, all red as it was, on his own finger. But his vengeance was unsatisfied. This man, normally animated by the noblest sentiments, had taken on the manners and the passions of a tiger. He fell upon the cadaver and his fingernails raked its scarcely-chilled flesh.

His *yataghan* was plunged into the Prince's heart three times over.

"For Mani Isacescu!" he howled, in a savage voice. "For Aurelio Comanescu! For Mar..."

He did not finish. The hiss of bullets was audible. Ioan slumped on top of the body of his enemy.

The following morning, when the Rumanian stretcher-bearers came to recover the wounded, Ioan Isacescu was still alive. He was taken to the ambulance; he had a bullet in his chest and another in his left knee; the latter could not be extracted.

A violent traumatic fever overwhelmed the wounded man; the physicians said that he would have to endure atrocious suffering. When typhus broke out in the hospital, Ioan was one of the first to be infected by it.

For three weeks, he was prey to the most intense delirium. The grimacing face of Boris Liatoukine never left his bedside. Captain Vampire's mutilated hand was suspended above the victim of hallucination, who believed that he could hear the sound of drops of blood falling upon his forehead one by one. Soon, the sheets, the curtain and everything else appeared red to him.

"Liatoukine!" he cried. "He's here! Chase him away!"

When he leapt from his bed, it took three strong men to wrestle the madman to the ground. His incessant cries disturbed the sleep of the other invalids, and he was relegated to a distant room. One night, it seemed to him that Captain Vampire cut off his little finger and tore away the copper ring. Then a gentler chimera came to abuse him: Mariora took him in her arms.

He regained command of his senses on All Saints' Day.

"Well, my lad," the medical orderly said to him, with a broad smile, "so we've finally woken up!"

Ioan looked up at the brave man. "The redoubt?" he stammered.

"What redoubt, my boy?"

"Gravitza."

"You're talking Ancient History! It's a long time since that was taken."

"Ah!" said Ioan, putting his hand over his yes, as if to collect his vague memories. After a pause, he added: "Where's Mitica Slobozianu?"

"What rank of officer is he, my son?"

"He's not an officer–he's a soldier."

"Oh, then we don't know," the fellow said, rearranging Ioan's pillows.

"And Prince Boris Liatoukine–where's he?"

The orderly squinted slyly. "Prince Liatoukine?" he repeated. "He's not dear to your heart, is he?"

"Who told you that?" cried Ioan, propping himself up on his elbow.

"You did, my boy. 'Liatoukine! He's here! Chase him away!' " The orderly imitated Ioan's distraught voice and gestures.

"But after all," the impatient *dorobantz*, "what's become of him?"

The orderly protruded his lower lip and slowly shook his head. "The crows that soar over Gravitza are the only ones who can tell you," he said. In a whisper, he added: "That's a blessing, too; Prince Liatoukine was an evil man."

These words were lost on Ioan. "Damn!" he cried, going slightly pale.

The copper ring was no longer on his finger.

"What a pity!" he said, after a moment's reflection. "Some *bashi-bazouk* must have stolen it." A bitter smile depressed the corners of his mouth. "And I'm not wearing it any longer!" he murmured.

## IX. Captain Vampire

"*Noël, Noël*, the Christ is born!" sang the silvery voices of the children parading an enormous decorative paper lantern through the city streets. The lantern was cut into the shape of a star and fixed to the end of a pole; it was supposed to represent the guiding star of the Oriental Kings. It projected a broad beam of blue-tinted light upon the thick snow that crackled rhythmically beneath the hurried footsteps of the little Magi.

The cold was very intense. The Russian wind, the *crivetzù*, had begun to blow, threatening from time to time to extinguish the star–to the great delight of the children, who huddled more urgently within their warm sheepskin coats, letting out little cries of joy and bursts of laughter. The young boyars clustered around Christmas trees loaded with splendid toys were certainly not laughing as heartily as these sons of peasants defending their paper lantern.

At last, that was the opinion of a man who was making painful progress along the Bucharest road. The unfortunate was lame in the left leg, walking with the aid of stick.

"I too used to sing, and I too used to laugh!" he sighed, sadly, as the little Rumanians passed him by. Abruptly, he pulled the peak of his cap over his eyes. Seeing a company of peasants on their way to a celebration, he left the path and slipped behind a stout oak. He did not want to be recognized. Alas, who could have guessed that, beneath the rags and tatters which scarcely covered the poor cripple's body, was Ioan Isacescu?

The *dorobantz*, whose wound still rendered him unfit for military service, had been sent back home. His home! When he had left it, young and full of hope, happiness and love, all prosperity had been resident there; he had come back disillusioned, prematurely aged, reckoning the past as a dream and refusing to believe in the future. What was he going to do in Baniassa? See Mariora again, hear her weep, forgive her and then marry her? No! He would seek out Old Mani and take him to Transylvania, where they would attempt to live, if not happily, at least in tranquillity.

"My father!" he murmured, in an affectionate tone, on finally seeing the paternal hut outlined in black against the snow-covered ground. "I still have my father! He's not expecting me. What a joy it will be for him–and what a consolation for me!" He raised his head, with a proud smile. "He'll ask me for his dagger," he continued. " 'Your dagger is at Gravitza,' I'll reply. 'Prince Liatoukine didn't want to give it back to me!' Father won't say anything, but he'll think that I've done well."

Ioan arrived in front of the cottage where his life had run so smoothly; his heart was beating violently and he paused to study it. There was not a glimmer of light in the windows, nor a wisp of smoke above the roof. The door was hermetically sealed. The hut had a sad and abandoned appearance–like that of the master who had returned to it.

"Father!" Ioan called, knocking gently on the door.

But there was no response.

*He's asleep*, Ioan thought. "Father!" he repeated, more loudly. "It's me, your son."

The same silence. Ioan was aware of his increasing anxiety.

"He must be here, though," he cried. With a vigorous kick, he forced the worm-eaten door open. He went in. The cottage's only room was empty; it was redolent with the acrid odor given off by old unused furniture and uninhabited apartments. He had no means of generating light, and set about exploring the room by touch. All the objects over which his fingers wandered were familiar; he recognized the little brass lamp, the sculpted frames of the holy images–everything, including the poor stool that was still set to the right-hand side of the misshapen table. These things were in their places, just as he had seen them in earlier times, but it seemed to his that they were covered in dust.

"My father's no longer here!" he cried, sorrowfully–and he slumped on to the stool. He put his head in his hands and remained motionless for some time. He did not think; he simply listened to the distant barking of guard-dogs.

Suddenly, he got up again. "I'm a fool," he said, in a firm and almost cheerful voice. "My father's at some neighbor's house, celebrating." He sang "*Noël, Noël,* the Christ is born!" in a falsetto voice, then added: "It's Christmas Eve–I'd forgotten that."

And he thought of Zamfira.

He readjusted the broken door as best he could, seized his staff and headed for Mozaïs' dwelling.

The father and the daughter were not there. Overcome by fatigue–the poor cripple had been walking all day and had scarcely eaten for two–and feeling more alone than before, he had reached that degree of exhaustion, more physical than mental, at which one can no longer aspire to anything but rest, wherever one might be. He lay down in the snow and closed his eyes.

He could not sleep; Mozaïs' hut was too close to the Slobozianu house. He wanted to see the threshold that he had worn never to cross again for one last time, but his half-frozen feet, clad in sandals worn down by Bulgarian soil, refused to carry him. He dragged himself along with his hands, bloodying his knees on stones rendered trenchant by the extreme cold.

When he perceived the windows that had once framed the elegant silhouette of Mariora so gracefully, he became almost afraid of finding something in his heart other than sentiments of disgust and indifference.

"It's finished," he murmured, laughing silently. "Ioan Isacescu no longer loves the mistress of Boris Liatoukine!"

He attempted to get up, in order to retreat more rapidly from a place whose appearance no longer invoked anything in him but shameful and unhappy memories. Suddenly, he shivered and lay down again in the snow, silently; a feminine shadow had just appeared on the doorstep.

"Wait for me, Father!" said a voice that was serious but soft. "I'll be back in a minute."

Ioan recognized that voice. "Zamfira! Zamfira!" he cried, reaching out towards the gypsy.

The sight of the black form crawling at her feet drew an exclamation of surprise from the young woman, who stepped backwards abruptly.

"Zamfira!" Ioan begged, lifting himself up on to is knees. "Zamfira, it's me–Ioan Isacescu!"

"Ioan!" she cried, launching herself toward him. Then she began jumping for joy and clapping her hands like a child, repeating: "Ioan's come back! Ioan's come back!"

"Too late!" murmured Ioan, sourly. He did not notice Zamfira's strange expression as her gaze seemed to search behind him for something that was not there.

She fell silent. Taking the *dorobantz*'s hand, affectionately, she sighed: "Poor Ioan. You know, then?"

"I know!" he exclaimed. "Shut up, Zamfira–don't speak her name!"

"Whose name?" Zamfira asked, astonished

"Whose name?" he repeated, forcefully. "Wretch! The infamous name–*her* name! I know everything, I tell you!"

"Alas!" Zamfira resumed, humbly. "Don't accuse her–rather pity her..."

"I despise her!" he cut in, with an explosion of anger.

"I'm more guilty than her," the gypsy went on, in tears. "It's my fault. She wanted to come back alone though Baniassa. A few thoughtless words she'd spoken, without meaning any harm, had offended my pride. I didn't want to follow her. Oh, I'm so sorry!" She drew him toward the house, adding: "Come with me, Ioan."

He recoiled sharply, withdrawing the hand that Zamfira had taken in her own. "No!" he cried, vehemently. "I'll never see her again. I don't know her any more. I don't love her any more! Do you hear, Zamfira? I don't love her any more!" He repeated the words with a ferocious laugh.

"The poor child isn't here," the gypsy murmured, shaking her head. "Living close to Baniassa became impossible for her. Sudden terrors seized her continually–the image of that man followed her everywhere. She called out for you incessantly in her delirium–you alone could defend her, she said. Oh, forgive her! If the ring..."

"Enough, Zamfira!" he cried, imperiously. "That creature is a stranger to me now. Stop your pleading–it's useless."

"Oh! My God!"

"I'm going away–far away," he continued, more calmly. "Some place where I'll be able to till soil that has never been dirtied by her impure contact. I shan't be taking any memory of her, or any love for her, with me. I'll pick up my old father and..."

"Your father?" Zamfira echoed, in sorrowful surprise.

"I'll pick up my father," Isacescu repeated. Then, he suddenly asked: "Where *is* my father?"

"What? You don't know? Your father..."

"Well, spit it out."

"He's dead."

"My father's dead!" he repeated, in a confirmatory tone. "I thought so." Gravely, he added: "Fortunate are the dead!" No tear glistened in his eye; he had scarcely any regret in his heart. Why should he weep? Who would he be mourning? Old Mani? Did he not envy the absence of thought and the eternal insensibility of the dead?

"Goodbye, Zamfira," he said, resolutely–but as he rapidly drew away, the gypsy's tremulous voice called out to him.

"Ioan!" she cried. "Where's Mitica?"

"I don't know," he replied, mechanically–and he disappeared into the swirling snow that the *crivetzù* was releasing upon the village.

He went straight to the cemetery, opened the gate–which was retained by a simple latch–and cried in a wild voice that resounded strangely in the silent night: "Rest in peace, Mani Isacescu! Your son has avenged you!"

For eight hours, Ioan lived like a pariah, dragging his misery through the splendors of Bucharest. Camp life had hardened him to corporeal suffering; he spent the night in a deserted alleyway were dogs were making rounds instead of patrols. When daylight came, he resumed his aimless wandering through the mazy streets.

He sought out the busiest places; the incessant hum of voices and the continual circulation of pedestrians eventually numbed the host of dark thoughts pressing upon him like a swarm of black butterflies behind his prematurely-wrinkled forehead.

Boyars and common people alike gazed at the crippled soldier with the tattered uniform and the scarred face, with respectful commiseration. Wretched as he was, he seemed to them to be greater than the *Domnù* himself; had he not shed his blood for the fatherland? Without any inkling of the naïve admiration that he excited, however, Ioan marched on and on, still fleeing from his memories.

One evening, he went to Philarete Station with the determined intention of rejoining his regiment in Bulgaria. The train was about to leave, and Ioan had to make an effort to place his left leg on the footplate of the carriage. Only then did the awareness of his infirmity come back to him.

"The fine crippled scout!" he cried, with bitter laugh, while the train steamed away in he direction of Giurgiu. He left the station, and, being thirsty, headed for the public fountain.

While he drank long draughts of icy water, a poorly-dressed little girl came up to him with her *cofitza*.[51] She raised her eyes timidly to the *dorobantz*, seemingly desirous of taking his place. With her disorderly blonde hair, the child reminded him of Mariora.

She went away trembling, with tears in her eyes and the empty jug in her hand.

"Hey, little girl!" said the soldier, ashamed of having allowed himself to be carried away by a ridiculous impulse of anger. "Come here. What's your name?"

His voice, suddenly softened, reassured the child, who came forward smiling.

"Sperantza," she replied.

"Sperantza!" Isacescu repeated, pensively. He filled the cofitza himself and slipped his entire fortune into Sperantza's fingers: a single *gologan*! [52] Then, without listening to the little girl's *multziani*,[53] he headed into the metropolis.

*I must put an end to this!* he said to himself. *I can't get that woman out of my head. I see her face everywhere, even in the features of an unknown child who doesn't resemble her at all. I feel that she's here, perhaps close by; I feel that I shan't have a moment's rest while that creature is alive. I've become feeble and cowardly. I...* He paused then went on, forcefully: *I've killed the lover; why haven't I killed the mistress?*

That same night, Zamfira's sleep was rudely interrupted by the sound of a clod of earth thudding into her window-pane; she got up hurriedly and thought she recognized Isacescu's voice calling to her.

"Is that you, Ioan?" she asked.

"Yes, it's me!" the *dorobantz* replied. He added, abruptly: "Where is she?"

"Mariora? In Bucharest, Strada Hagielor, No. 8," said Zamfira, in a single breath. She joined her hands together and went on: "May Heaven bless you, Ioan Isacescu! You're going to do a good deed."

*May Heaven pardon me!* he thought. *I'm going to commit a crime!*

The next day was January 1. The Sun rose splendidly into a clear sky and spangled the silvered cupolas of the churches with its golden rays. The breeze seemed a mere caress, and flocks of wild sparrows were twittering gaily as they pecked at the grain which the Rumanians had not neglected to sew on the thresholds of their houses, in order to attract prosperity of every sort. An air of happiness and contentment that one scarcely ever saw in Bucharest any longer blossomed again in the faces of the early risers. One might have thought that everything was smiling and welcoming the new year–which would, they hoped, be less fateful than its immediate predecessor.

While the city awoke around him, Ioan was leaning on the balustrade of the Vacaresci Bridge; he was contemplating, with a typical Eastern European vagueness of expression, the little blue waves of the Dimbovitza lapping against the sparse grass on its banks. He was holding his combat revolver negligently in his right hand, when a sudden twitch of his arm caused him to drop it into the river. At the same time, a child's voice beside him murmured: *Bunà zioa, frate*.[54]

Ioan recognized Sperantza. The little girl's friendly greeting touched him. He groaned weakly, but the combined influences of the beautiful sky–which had been cloudy for such a long time–and the solemn festivities of the day had reopened his heart to generous emotion. He remembered that Mariora had once said to him: "If I were ever unfaithful, Ionitza you would surely kill me with your big sword...me, and the other?"

"You, no–the other, certainly," he had replied.

Liatoukine was dead; Ioan would spare Mariora.

*A crime always seeks its criminal!* [55] he said to himself. *Isacescu has never been the name of a murderer.* He picked Sperantza up and hugged her fervently.

"My friend," she said, "you're hurting me." She adopted a serious attitude, which contrasted with her usual pert expression, and went on: "I like you a lot. Where are you going? I'll go with you."

"Where am I going, my poor child? Alas, I don't know that myself!"

Sperantza opened her eyes wide. "Haven't you got a house?" she said.

"Not any longer."

"Your father? Your mother?"

Ioan shook his head.

"They've been put in the ground, haven't they?" she said, gravely. "That's because they're dead, my friend."

"Yes, they're dead," Ioan repeated, mechanically.

Sperantza had an idea. "Come with me," she said. "I'll take you home." She added, by way of explanation: "It's not very big, but you don't take up much room."

"May God protect you, Sperantza," he said, tenderly. "Wherever you're going, I'll go!"

Sperantza seized his hand. He let himself be guided by her, happy to follow her and hear her chatter. Sperantza immediately began to tell her story. Her mother made flowers for the shops in the Strada Mogosoi; her father worked at the gasworks; they were poor; they had once been rich, before they came to Bucharest. Sperantza had been born "on the other side of the mountains;" she could read and write, well enough to count and manage the household budget, even though she was only seven. She had a bird, a dog "of her very own," and she also had a friend. "A grown-up friend!" she said, with proud satisfaction.

As they turned into the Strada Tarieri, Ioam suddenly stopped. "Where are you going, Sperantza my darling?" he said.

"Home, my friend. Strada Hagielor, No. 8," the little girl replied, trying to drag Ioan onwards. "Jesus Christ! How pale you are! Are you ill?"

"No. But, Sperantza, your father and mother aren't the only people who live in that house..."

"Certainly not, my friend. There's Mariora Slobozianu, who..."

"Mariora Slobozianu!"

"Do you know her? She's my grown-up friend! She's very beautiful. Come on, I'll show her to you."

Profoundly disturbed by the effect that Sperantza's words had had on him, Ioan understood that his old love was not yet extinct in his heart, and that it would only require Mariora to look at him to dissipate is anger.

"No, Sperantza," he said, in a barely-intelligible voice. "I won't see her!"

"Why not?" the little girl persisted. "She'll like you just as much I do. Besides, didn't you say that wherever I was going, you..."

"That's true!" Ioan said, interrupting her. Sperantza had rendered him as fatalistic as a Muslim. *Let's go!* he thought, as he walked slowly beside the little girl, who led him along the Strada Hagielor. *What must be, must be!*

Sperantza's house was a Byzantine construction, of a sort still found in the quainter quarters of Bucharest. Ioan and his guide went through a narrow passageway, which ended in a square courtyard planted with box-trees and holly bushes.

"Wait!" said Ioan to Sperantza, as she was about to run to her mother to announce the arrival of a new guest. "Take me to...your grown-up friend."

Sperantza obeyed, and Ioan climbed the frail spiral staircase that led to Mariora's room, with a firm tread.

"She's in here," said the child, pointing to a door painted rose-pink. "Shhh! She's talking–listen!"

"No, Baba Sophia," said a voice that reminded the *dorobantz* of an era of lost happiness, "I'll only go back there when Ioan comes back."

"Ioan," whispered Sperantza, "is the name of a soldier she loves and who'll marry her when the war is over."

Ioan dated sideways glance at the child. "She loves this soldier, you say?"

"And how! She never wants to talk about anything but him."

"You know, little one," he said, with an ironic smile, "This Ioan–it's me."

"You!" Sperantza bounded towards the rose-pink door.

Ioan held her back. "Leave me alone, now," he said to her. "I've a great many things to say to Mariora."

Sperantza, who was neither obstinate nor curious, ran down the stairs, letting out little cries of joy.

Ioan did not want to give himself time to reflect. The key turned in the lock; he went in.

"Isacescu!" said Baba Sophia.

"Ionitza!" cried Mariora.

Two bare arms slid around his neck; a flood of blonde hair inundated his shoulders and ardent kisses were showered upon his forehead. In the middle of the room, Baba Sophia was kneeling down, praying fervently.

*She embraced Liatoukine thus!* Ioan said to himself. That thought brought all his hatred flooding back.

"Get away!" he said. "Get away, vile creature!" And, seizing a handful of Mariora's loose hair, he forced her to look him in the face. "Vile creature!" he repeated. Then he threw the poor stupefied girl across the room.

Baba Sophia leapt to her feet like a tigress. "Wretch!" she yelped. "How dare you...?"

Mariora clapped her hand over the old woman's furiously-pursed lips. "Be quiet, godmother," she begged. "Ioan is mad!"

"Mad!" he murmured, taking a step towards her "Yes, I was, when I believed your words and your sworn promises, which were nothing but perjury–when I allowed myself to be abused by your caresses, which only served to better hide your perfidies! I was mad when I loved you, Mariora! Now...I know...I've seen...!"

"Oh, my God!" sobbed the young woman. "But what have I done?"

Baba Sophia, her patience exhausted, put her arms behind her back and said to Ioan, with false calmness: "Listen, Corporal Isacescu–if you've only come here to reel off pleasantries of that sort. my opinion is that it's a great pity that you didn't stay where you were, like so many brave boys of greater worth than you!"

"Then you're a worthy accomplice of the other one," retorted Ioan, paying no heed to the gorgon's invective. "He too asked me what he had done. Do you know how I replied to him, Mariora?"

"Ioan," cried the priest's daughter, grabbing the *dorobantz*'s hand.

"Get away, I tell you," he repeated. With insulting sarcasm, he added: "Do you take me for Boris Liatoukine?"

135

"Boris Liatoukine!" Mariora repeated, slowly. "I don't know him."

"Oh? You don't know Boris Liatoukine–the man with the yellow eyes from the Baniasa Woods?"

Mariora shuddered. "Indeed, my Ionitza," she replied, tremulously. "I dream about him, I..."

Ioan interrupted her in a thunderous voice. "Your hand! Show me your hand!"

Mariora mechanically exposed both hands to the pitiless gaze of the *dorobantz*.

"And the ring?" he said.

"The ring?" Mariora stammered, quite beside herself. "Yes...that's true. He took it, my love–he took it!"

"Ah! You finally admit it!" he cried, with a bitter laugh. "He took it!"

"I couldn't...Ionitza!" Her tears were choking her; she covered her head with her apron. "All this because the ring is lost!" she groaned.

"It was only copper anyway, your ring!" the terrible godmother resumed. "We're only talking about your peddler's trinkets! Leave my god-daughter be. She's much too beautiful for a cripple like you. If you no longer want her, just tell her straight out, without such jeremiads! We'll have suitors flocking round, of better quality than the son of *your* father!"

Baba Sophia paused to draw breath.

"Me, marry Boris Liatoukine's mistress!" Ioan cried, indignantly. "You're dreaming, old woman!"

At these words Mariora raised her head again; her tears drying up, she advanced towards Ioan and stood before her fiancé, cold and pale. "I don't understand," she said, softly.

"You're the mistress of Boris Liatoukine," Ioan repeated, harshly. "Do you dare to deny that it's true, wretch?"

"The mistress..." Mariora stammered, astounded. She leaned on the back of a chair for support; her lips were pale, her eyes lit up. "Who told you that?" she demanded, quivering.

"Liatoukine himself."

"He lied!" she cried, in a voice vibrant with anger. "He lied!" she repeated, going to the gilded frame that enclosed a richly-illuminated representation of the Virgin. "I swear before these holy images."

"Which tells you that he lied!" Baba Sophia added, having recovered her breath. "Where do you get these fine notions, eh? To set about slandering the honor of honest women! It'll be a fine day when a beardless adolescent can come preaching morality to old Sophia! Haven't I always set the little one the strictest example of virtue? There's plenty in the village can remind you of that if you've forgotten."

"I don't believe you, Mariora Slobozianu," Ioan murmured, without raising his eyes.

Mariora made an effort to hold back her tears. Meekly, she presented her forehead for the *dorobantz* to kiss. In a voice stifled by sorrow, she said: "Goodbye, then, my beloved–and may the Supreme Lord pardon you, as I do!"

Ioan did not budge. *If Liatoukine lied!* he thought. *Oh, that would be Heaven!* "I want to believe you, Mariora," he said, "but...I saw that ring on Liatoukine's finger.

"It was in the Baniassa Woods," Mariora replied, simply. "We were alone: he took my ring."

"And afterwards?"

137

"That's all!"

"That man would not have spared you!" he said, shaking his head.

"Listen," she said, lowering her voice mysteriously. "That man is not a man: he's a vampire. He has two pupils in each eye. His gaze puts you into a strange sleep that ends in death. The saints were protecting me from the heights of Heaven: midnight chimed, a cock crew in the distance... What could he do to me then?"

Although belief in vampirism and the evil eye did not appear to him to be indisputable articles of faith, Ioan considered Mariora's bizarre explanation as the sole ray of light that might dissipate the grey shadows among which his hope was lost. Mariora innocent–that was the future clarified, happiness restored, life with all the joys that make all sorrows supportable.

The dignified attitude and limpid gaze of his fiancée succeeded in convincing him. "Then...it isn't true?" he said.

"It isn't true," Mariora repeated, forcefully.

While they stood there side by side, embarrassed and hesitant, Baba Sophia cried: "There we go! It's all over! Corporal Isacescu, should we send for the priest? Yes or no?"

"Get on with it, Baba Sophia!" Ioan replied, gaily, taking Mariora in his arms. "If your legs are as agile as your tongue, it'll soon be done!"

"Corporal Isacescu," Baba Sophia replied, putting her stiff hand on the *dorobantz*'s shoulder, "I forgive you for all the villainous things you said to me." And, abandoning herself unreservedly to exuberant joy, the old godmother began capering around the room like a mad goat, while Mariora, kneeling before the holy images, gave thanks to the Lord.

Happy people have no history. The happiness of the two fiancés was not quite complete. The memory of Mitica soared like a black bird above their dovecote. Ioan made several trips to the Ministry of War, but when the officials learned that Mitica Slobozianu was only a simple soldier, they replied: "Ah, then we don't know," like the medical orderly at Pleven.

Ioan persuaded Zamfira that Mitica was a prisoner in Constantinople and that he would come back as soon as the peace treaty was signed. People easily believe what they wish to believe, and every night, as she went to sleep, Zamfira told herself that the following day would bring him back.

How many times had Ioan to start the story of his adventures all over again? Mariora never tired of hearing him relate the moving scenes of the taking of Gravitza; the sad demise of the boyar Relia, "who only talked about wine and maize," brought tears to her eyes, and when it was a question of Liatoukine's death, she kissed the hand that had embedded the dagger in the breast of the man with yellow eyes.

Now that Captain Vampire was no more, the thickets of the Baniassa Woods had lost the ability to terrify the priest's daughter, and the proposal that she should return to the village was accepted unanimously.

The month of January was taken up with preparations of every sort. It was decided that the newlyweds would live in he Slobozianus' house, and Mariora sent to Bucharest for a quantity of useless items of furniture that were necessary to her, and which cluttered very corner. Baba Sophia complained of the abomination. Enough wardrobes to contain the linen of 20 families! Enough chairs to seat the entire National Assembly! In her day people had thought themselves lucky to be able to squat on a smooth floor!–and so on. To which Mariora replied that the past was the past, that one could stuff drawers full of fine linen and invite the mayor to dinner.

The marriage date was irrevocably fixed as February 15.

On the evening before, while Ioan was waiting in the office of an advocate in the city, to whom Old Mani had entrusted his money, Zamfira and Mariora were busy arranging the latter's trousseau: aprons with multicolored stripes, richly-embroidered bodices and gold-spangled waistbands all dazzled the eyes of the enraptured Baba Sophia. "Princess Elisabeth would look like a bourgeois next to you, my girl," she said to the future Madame Isacescu–who, bustling about and scuttling like a mouse, replied to her godmother's admiring comments with loud peals of laughter.

Three curt raps on the entrance-door caused a scalloped skirt to fall from Mariora's hands. Who could it be at this late hour? Mariora, whose particular memories rendered her less than valiant, took refuge in the thin arms of the worthy Sophia, who was rooted to the spot. Zamfira took it upon herself, as usual, to act.

The frail staircase groaned beneath a heavy and measured tread. The door of the room opened noisily and the gypsy reappeared, leading a man of tall stature and stern features, wearing a Cossack uniform.

It did not require much to reawaken Mademoiselle Slobozianu's old terrors. The young woman's fear reached its peak when the Russian came towards her and, greeting her by name, presented her with a large oblong box studded with iron nails and carefully sealed. Mariora, pale with fright, backed up against the wall.

"What is it?" asked Zamfira, bravely taking the box from the hands of the singular messenger.

The Cossack made a gesture to signify that he did not understand; the gypsy translated the question into Russian.

"A wedding gift," replied the Cossack, heading for the door.

"And from whom does it come?" Zamfira persisted.

"Forbidden to say!" the incorruptible courier said, laconically, as he disappeared down the stairs.

"There's some devilment in there!" said Baba Sophia, shaking her head. "That box has a suspicious appearance. If you'll take my advice, little one, you'll only open it in the presence of your husband."

Mariora's apprehension overcame her curiosity; she praised her godmother's foresight, and the three women spend the rest of the evening formulating and tearing apart the most improbable conjectures. The mysterious box, which was quite heavy, was weighed up, turned round and sounded out. At the least agitation a clinking noise could be heard, as if a metal object were clinking against the walls of the coffer; then the ear perceived another, fainter noise, like a coin brushing against the wood. The box evidently contained two objects.

Mariora slept badly; she dreamed all night of serpents escaping from a half-open casket, hissing as they did so. When Ioan came, before dawn, to visit his future spouse in private, Baba Sophia gave him a voluble account of the previous evening's incident, not without spicing her recitation with dramatic details that were very stimulating to the imagination.

Ioan had the box brought to him, and introduced a hook into the lock. In response to the instrument's efforts, the cover sprang open.

A quadruple cry of amazement went up. The box contained Mariora's copper ring and Old Mani's *yataghan*. The ring was completely oxidized and a thick layer of rust covered the knife's blade, but the name of its owner–*Mani Isacescu*–was still legible, crudely engraved on the horn handle.

"There!" said Baba Sophia, triumphantly. "Didn't I tell you that the Devil was inside!"

The entire village was present at the wedding feast, which went admirably well, thanks to the culinary talents of Baba Sophia, who surpassed herself.

Sperantza's mother had taken charge of Mariora's dress, and the latter, who doted on western fashions, had replaced the crown of boxwood that traditionally adorns the heads of Walachian winter brides with a magnificent garland of orange-blossom–which she wore proudly, as she had the right to do.

Little Ralitza made the whispered observation that the married couple did not seem very joyful.

"Hold your malicious tongue," said one of her neighbors. "The grass hasn't yet grown over his father's grave and her brother is probably in the arms of the world's bride."[56]

Even so, Ralitza's observation was not without justice. Mariora kept her eyes perpetually lowered, and scarcely made any reply to the conventional pleasantries addressed to her from all sides of the table. Ioan contemplated the Greek wine in his glass with a bleak expression; through the gilded liquid he could distinctly see Liatoukine stretched out on the ground, white-faced, with a dagger stuck in his breast.

"Well?" said Madame Isacescu, interrogatively, when the two spouses finally found themselves alone.

"Listen, darling," said the ex-*dorobantz*. "One of the man's friends must have read our name on the dagger's hilt and sent it back to me."

"That's possible," Mariora said. "But what about the ring?" she added, shaking her head.

"Ah, the ring...that's true!" Ioan murmured, disconcerted. Then, embracing his wife affectionately, he said, suggestively: "Tell me, Mariora, whether we really have to think about this today?"

Mariora smiled, and they gave it no further thought.

The days went by uniformly and rapidly for the two newlyweds. Ioan, for the sake of his peace of mind, had given up trying to find the key to the enigma represented by the ring and the dagger, but Mariora, who was fearful that the presence of the accursed objects might bring them bad luck, confided her anxieties to Baba Sophia.

"We should throw this rubbish in the Dimbovitza," the duenna said to Ioan.

He refused. Putting the things carefully away in a drawer, he said: "It's important to keep them."

The repeated insistences of the godmother were reinforced by the supplications of he god-daughter, who declared that she would only feel perfectly happy when the ring and the *yataghan* were gone. Ioan was even more fearful of Baba Sophia's nagging than his wife's tears; he consented to bury the box, the ring and the dagger in a deserted spot in the Baniassa woods. Baba Sophia shut up, Mariora recovered her smile, and everyone thought that they would be liberated forever from the odious memory of Captain Vampire.

Mitica's absence being indefinitely prolonged, Ioan resolved to approach the Minister of War directly. An audience was immediately granted, and Mariora asked her husband for permission to accompany him. While putting on her best clothes, Madame Isacescu delighted herself with the thought of being able to repeat to her astounded neighbors: "The minister asked us...the minister replied to us..." and so on. And when Baba Sophia had cast a final eye over Mariora's costume, the two young spouses took the road to the city.

A spring breeze was floating in the air. April had reddened the chilly buds peeping timidly outside their envelopes. Storks and swallows were flying overhead, and violets embalmed the silken grass, in which the eye searched vainly for the humblest of flowers: the white daisy, which is not common in Rumania.

Mariora and Ioan were walking side by side in silence, fearful that words might disturb the gentle ecstasy that the spring morning had poured into their souls, when the advance sentinel of renewal suddenly released its dutiful signal, a joyful "cuckoo!"

Since the adventure of the Baniassa Woods, Mariora had sworn an implacable hatred for the avian omen that had never promised her anything but misfortune, but Ioan did not partake of his wife's prejudice.

Well, *ibita mea*," he said, teasing her gently, "what does the bird say?"

"It doesn't say anything," she replied, with all the seriousness in the world. "It's neither to our right nor to our left–it's over there, in front of us. Do you see it flying away?"

"And that signifies...?"

"Nothing–absolutely nothing. Don't laugh," she added. "That song reminds me of terrible moments, and that bird has always been the precursor, for me...of Liatoukine."

"But, since Liatoukine is dead..."

A gesture from Mariora cut Ioan's words short. "Let's never speak of that man again, Ionitza," she said.

Eleven o'clock was chiming as they arrived in Bucharest. The minister's office did not open until noon. As they went along the Strada Mogosoi, Mariora, who felt obliged to erase the disagreeable impression the encounter with the cuckoo had made on her, suggested that they visit the Sarindar Church. A marriage was being celebrated there–a boyar marriage, at which there would be splendid ladies' dresses, and officers' uniforms making up the couple's cortège, in the presence of the metropolitan Archbishop, who was officiating in person.

*A good omen!* Mariora thought, reassured. *We'll see Mitica again.*

Dragging Ioan through he crowd of spectators who were filling the church, she got a position as close as she could to the *catapeteasma*–the icon-adorned door separating the nave from the bema. From where they were, neither Ioan nor Mariora could see the faces of the bride and groom. In any case, the bride's beauty was of scant importance to Madame Isacescu, who only had eyes for the white satin dress, ornamented with lace and rivulets of jewels. The ex-*dorobantz*'s gaze never left the groom. That tall figure, that stiff stance and, above all, that uniform, were not unfamiliar to Isacescu.

"Where have I seen that man before?" he asked himself, waiting impatiently for the officer to turn around.

The ceremony was marked by a rather amusing incident. A political–one might almost say historic–person of note had been charged with holding the nuptial crown suspended above the bride's head, as is the custom in Orthodox marriages. The bride was tall; the statesman was short. The latter, feeling that his gravity was com-

145

promised, was standing on tiptoe and making desperate efforts to maintain his balance, to his own embarrassment and the extreme joy of the jeering public, which no longer idolized him.

"Who's getting married, then?" Mariora asked a woman of the people, who was chattering much more freely than the sanctity of the location should have permitted.

"Jesus Christ, little mother! You're obviously not from the city, to ask me a question like that! No one's talked about anything except this marriage for a month. I don't suppose they adore one another like turtle-doves, but *he* has two million rubles, and the good graces of the Russian Emperor; *she* owns lots and lots of land...it goes on forever."

"But who...?" Mariora persisted.

"I'm getting there, chicken. Prince Androcles Comanescu is marrying his daughter Epistimia to General Boris Liatoukine, so they say."

"That's not true!" Ioan retorted, forcefully. "Boris Liatoukine is dead!"

"Oh yes?" the old woman sniggered. "You're soft in the head, my lad! Dead! The dead aren't so hearty!"

The ceremony finished as the shrew pronounced these words, and the married couple, followed by their cortège, headed slowly towards the exit door, which was wide open.

Mariora fell unconscious into her husband's arms.

Next to Epistimia, who was moving forwards haughtily and scornfully, marched Boris Liatoukine, in the grandiose uniform of a Russian general: Boris Liatoukine, who was said to have died at Gravitza on September 11, 1877, Saint Alexander's Day!

Hardly having the strength to support Mariora, the motionless Ioan–his mouth agape, his eyebrows bristling and his eyes haggard–was the personification of Terror.

Captain Vampire's clothing brushed against Ioan's. The resurrected man's eyes flared; his ironic smile became ferocious; he raised his gloveless right hand.

The little finger had been cut off at the third knuckle!

Then the cortège continued on its way; the church emptied little by little, and complete silence was re-established.

"I killed him, though!" murmured the paralyzed Ioan. "I'm sure that I killed him!"

Eight hours later, Domna Epistimia was dead, and the Isacescu family, abandoning Baniassa forever, moved to Craiova.

## *Epilogue*

Ioan Isacescu became what one might appropriately call a prosperous landowner. The reasonably large sum amassed by his father permitted him to acquire 15 *pogones* of arable land in the vicinity of Craiova, which he cultivated himself. His wife's wealth was invested advantageously, and all his tenants said that, if all its landlords acted as fairly as "the cripple," Rumania would be one of the most delightful places in this wretched world.

Ioan, believing that "it is only to see that masters have eyes," still traveled to Baniassa once a month. Mariora never thought of accompanying him. She had sworn to die without ever seeing Bucharest again. She made the sign of the cross at the merest clink of a Russian spur; the sight of a Cossack caused her to fall in a faint. Ioan had forbidden everyone to mention the name of Liatoukine in front of her. She had learned to cook *mamaliga* and to make cheese; she did not gossip with the neighbors, for which her husband praised her a great deal, and she had no more bitter words for Zamfira, who had brought her father to live with her in Craiova.

No news had ever been received of Mitica. Zamfira remained unmarried; her red ribbons faded to yellow. She brought up Mariora's children.

Baba Sophia grumbled and stormed all day long; she was forgiven her continual nagging on account of her age.

Old Mozaïs was completely senile; he spent entire hours crouched on his doorstep, incessantly murmuring "Serban Yezidee! Serban Yezidee!" while shaking his head. Then he suddenly got up and grabbed his staff.

"Where are you going, father?" his daughter asked him. "To Smyrna!" he replied, in a firm voice. He took a few steps outside, then came back to lie down in the dust, repeating his terrible refrain: "Serban Yezidee!"

Domna Agapia ended up marrying the 8,000 hectares of young Decebale Privighetoareano. Decebale shuttled back and forth between Bucharest and Paris, beat the Princess, debauched her chambermaids and bought diamonds for pretty ballerinas. Mademoiselle Comanescu wepts night and day; she became very thin, and when she threatened to return to her father, Decebale offered her his arm to take her to the railway station. She then became a permanently resident in Vienna, where luck reacquainted her with her blue-eyed dancer, Igor Moïleff, who carried an interesting wound very gracefully. He desired to console Madame Privighetoareano. The poor Princess was deeply perplexed; Decebale, willingly excusing his own peccadilloes, showed himself to be not at all indulgent of his wife's.

The Comanescu Palace became the terrestrial paradise of priests, igumens [57] and Archimandrites, who always found a good meal, good lodgings and a cash donation there. Domna Rosanda threw herself wholeheartedly into devotion; the rosary replaced the fan between her fingers; she wore somber dresses, spoke through her nose and planned to build a church.

Androcles alone was happy. He had shed two tears over the graves of Aurelio and Epistimia. "We are all mortal!" he said, with an appropriate delicacy. Then he passed the back of his hand over his moist eyelids and returned to his business affairs. He constructed a sugar refinery in the Vlasca district, which formed a counterpart to his wife's church. In the Senate, he featured among the mute orators. His glory was at its apogee; the

Order of the Rumania Star was conferred upon him, at the same time as the confectioner Capsa and the brewer Opler, two persons well-known in Bucharest.[58]

As for Boris Liatoukine, he paraded his insolence in the drawing-rooms of St Petersburg again. All the talk was of his strange adventure. The ladies bemoaned the fate of the unfortunate Princess Liatoukine—the third of that name—and not one aspired to succeed her. The superstitious old dowagers claimed that Prince Boris was well and truly slain at Gravitza; the Liatoukine whom the Tsar has elevated to the rank of General was, according to them, merely the Prince's cadaver, temporarily reanimated by a breath of infernal life.

Some of Captain Vampire's friends attempted to solve the mystery. Misfortune overtook them all.

Liatoukine challenged Bogomil Tchestakoff and struck him dead.

Stenka Sokolich, wrongly suspected of producing nihilist propaganda, was deported to Siberia.

Yuri Levine was stripped of his rank; he was rumored to have gone insane.

## *Afterword*

Matei Cazacu's argument for the possible influence of *Le Capitaine Vampire* on Bram Stoker's *Dracula* cites several points of allegedly significant coincidence: its central character is a male aristocrat; he possesses hypnotic powers of subjection; and he attacks the fiancée of the hero, whose friend also has a fiancée. Cazacu also notes that Stoker's brother had served as a physician in the Turkish army that fought in Bulgaria during the Russo-Turkish war, suggesting that this might have played a part in attracting Stoker's attention to the novella.

Cazacu alleges that this pattern of coincidences is striking, but if one bears in mind that it mostly reproduces features already present in Polidori and Dumas–with whose works Stoker is far more likely to have been familiar–the coincidences become much more trivial. What is much more striking, in fact, is the collection of traits attributed to Boris Liatoukine that are *not* replicated in *Dracula*, and which contrast with much other vampire fiction.

It appears that the only victims who reputedly perish at Liatoukine's hands–allegedly bearing "the mark of the vampire" on their necks, although they are rumored to have died of strangulation rather than exsanguination–are his three wives. (Stoker's Dracula has three "brides" too, but Liatoukine's have all been legitimately married to him in church, and none is resurrected from the dead.) Liatoukine's other rumored seductions seem to be perfectly ordinary seductions, if they are to be counted as seductions at all; those of which we catch a glimpse are more like rapes. While Stoker's Dracula–contrary to the supposition inherited by his successors–can operate in daylight if necessary, he definitely has a strong affinity for the night; Boris Liatoukine, on the other hand, seems perfectly comfortable by day and night alike–a necessary facility for an army Colonel on active service.

Given this, it is not at all obvious that, in *Le Capitaine Vampire*, what Marie Nizet understood by the word "vampire" had anything much in common with what Bram Stoker and his myriad imitators were to understand by it. We are now accustomed, largely thanks to Stoker, to thinking that *the* definite feature of vampirism is a taste for and dependency on human blood, but that is not at all obvious in the texts to which Nizet is most likely to have referred before writing her novel, where bitten throats are either absent or cited only as incidental features in accounts of malevolent sexual predation. Boris Liatoukine is certainly not dependent on human blood, shows no obvious attraction to it or appetite for it, and no firm evidence is presented in the novella that he ever drinks anyone's blood at all. Indeed, his reputation as a vampire–particularly the anecdote that allegedly led to the acquisition of his nickname–seems to be solely dependent on his corpse-like appearance and his apparent ability to return from the dead. Even his possession of the power of the evil eye, and his supposed ability to be in two places at once, seem largely incidental.

If one allows for a certain understandable exaggeration in the stories told by his Russian acolytes, the only firm evidence presented in the story for Liatoukine's ability to return from the dead is his reappearance in Bucharest after having been slain by Ioan Isacescu. Having done that, however, Isacescu immediately falls into a hallucinatory delirium precipitated by his bullet-wounds, and it is not inconceivable that his act of vengeance was an aspect of that hallucination rather than a real event; Liatoukine's behavior, especially in making no attempt to defend himself, certainly seems sufficiently peculiar to belong to a dream–although his carelessness in the face of death has already been mentioned.

The fact that Liatoukine's behavior seems equally odd on other occasions may indicate that there is something *essentially* hallucinatory about him, even though so many people are aware of his existence; it is not at all clear how the reader ought to construe the slightly paradoxical aspects of his behavior in respect of both Mariora and Relia. In the latter case, his behavior seems as much voyeuristic as directly threatening. The former incident is even more peculiar. Did Liatoukine really refrain from raping Mariora after playing the Big Bad Wolf to her Little Red Riding-Hood, as Mariora insists? If he did refrain, did he really do it for the reason she proffers? Did he ever intend to rape her, given that her retrospective account of her first meeting with him implies that what would actually have happened, had Relia not interrupted their *tête-à-tête*, is that she would have perished under the gaze of his remarkable eyes?

In a sense, the most puzzling aspect of Ioan Isacescu's vendetta against Liatoukine is the manner in which it is compounded during their second encounter. How does Liatoukine know that Ioan is Mariora's fiancé–how does he even know Mariora's name–if her account of what happened in the woods is true? The reader can understand readily enough how Liatoukine's acolytes are able pick up the cue he gives them and play the cruel game of "Oh, *I* know Mariora"–but how does he know, when he is challenged to confirm or deny their story, what impact the sight of the ring will have on the tormented *dorobantz*? Perhaps he knows these things because he is the Devil's agent, and is thus privy to information irrecoverable by natural means–but exactly what sort of a game is he playing with Isacescu, and why? Why does he take the trouble to send the rusty dagger and thoroughly oxidized ring back to Isacescu and Mariora as a "wedding present?" Something is obviously not quite right here, and it seems quite possible that one component of that unrightness is that poor Isacescu is not quite right in the head. Is it possible that none of Isacescu's confrontations with Liatoukine actually happened in the way the narrative voice says that they did?

The most probable solution to these conundrums is that the 19-year-old writer simply did not have full control of her materials, and could not make up her own mind exactly what had actually happened in her story or exactly what kind of monster Boris Liatoukine actually was. Whether that is so or not, though, the story certainly makes more sense if Liatoukine is considered to be the symbolic evil genius of the Russian army; effective in different ways in different places–including different places at the same time–and not a mere person at all. It is worth remembering that Liatoukine first appears in direct response to a formal curse uttered by Isacescu's father against the Russian invaders, and also how Yuri Levine sums him up in the chapter that claims to explain what he is: "Liatoukine is everywhere...he has the gift of ubiquity, just like the good God."

If Liatoukine is seen as a symbolic incarnation of the Russians' guiding spirit, his conduct towards Isa-cescu becomes a materialization of the contemptuous attitude and voice of the Russian nation and army to the Rumanian nation and army, mocking the Rumanians' conviction that they were cynically and cruelly used when they were ordered to lead the attack on Gravitza and bear the brunt of the defensive fire. Isacescu's response would then be equally symbolic–and it is not at all surprising that the evil genius survives the act of revenge, going on to commit further mocking atrocities, within the Russian ranks as well as without.

It seems to me, in consequence of the sum of these observations and arguments, that it is unlikely that Bram Stoker ever read *Le Captaine Vampire*–and, more importantly, that even if he did, he did not take any substantial influence specifically therefrom. That does not mean, however, that *Le Capitaine Vampire* is not a significant work in the history of vampire fiction; it clearly is–but it owes that distinction to its own imaginative qualities, not to any influence it might have had. It is undoubtedly one of the finest literary works ever to have made use of the vampire motif, because rather than despite the fact that its usage was highly idiosyncratic and probably purely symbolic.

After making such a spectacular start as a writer of fiction, one might have expected Marie Nizet to build a solid literary career, but she did not. Cazacu records that she was "briefly" married to "a certain Mercier" but that she wrote nothing after the marriage, although she did not die until 1922. Cazacu also records, however, that her brother Henri made the actual pilgrimage that she could not, setting off for Rumania in 1883–at the age of 19–and working there as tutor for several years. His first book, published in that year, must have been completed before he left Brussels, and was a Naturalist account of life in that city, *Bruxelles rigole; moeurs exotiques* [The Brussels Gutter: Exotic Mores]. Like his sister, though, Henri found difficulty in extrapolating his literary career. Cazacu claims that his second novel, *Les Béotiens* [metaphorically, The Philistines] (1885), caused considerable offence among the members of the literary community pilloried therein.

Henri Nizet's final novel, *Suggestion* (1891), anticipated George du Maurier's *Trilby* (1894) in presenting an account of hypnotic domination, but incorporated a crucial homoerotic element that recalls Boris Liatoukine's treatment of Relia Comanescu in *Le Capitaine Vampire*. Although the dominator in Henri's novel is a Frenchman, Paul Lebarrois, his male victim, Séphorah, is a Rumanian; unsurprisingly, the metaphor of vampiric predation is elaborately deployed, as it was later to be in George Viereck's similarly homoerotic account of psychic domination, *The House of the Vampire* (1907). If, as Cazacu blithely states, *Suggestion* really was an "autobiographical novel," it may shed new light on the inspiration for the remarkable chapter in his sister's novella describing Relia's awful experience in the hands of the Russian officers.

Henri evidently took the theme of *Suggestion* very seriously; his only substantial publication thereafter was *L'Hypnotisme, étude critique* [Hypnotism: A Critical Study] in 1893. The coincidences of theme between *Dracula* and *Suggestion* are, as in the case of *Le Capitaine Vampire*, more easily explained as a matter of the common influence of other texts than by any direct transmission of ideas from the former to the latter.

Cazacu is certainly correct, however, to observe that the story of Henri Nizet's literary career is a fascinating addendum to the story of Marie's, and may offer significant clues regarding the origin of the remarkable undercurrents of feeling submerged within *Le Capitaine Vampire*.


Brian Stableford

# *Notes*

Notes that merely translate footnotes from the original text are indicated by the addendum [Nizet]; in cases where I have added a further annotation of my own, my own comments are placed after that credit.

---

[1] Available from Black Coat Press as *Lord Ruthven the Vampire* (IBN 978-1-932983-10-4) and *The Return of Lord Ruthven* (ISBN 978-1-932983-11-1).

[2] Available from Black Coat Press as *Vampire City* (ISBN 978-0-9740711-6-9).

[3] One of the victims of the collapse was Paul Féval, who had–astonishingly as well as unwisely–gambled his entire fortune on the investment.

[4] This reference is to Ion Heliade Radulescu (see the introduction).

[5] Varzin was Bismarck's country estate in Pomerania.

[6] *Raki* is here defined as plum brandy [Nizet], although the term is often used more generally to refer to strong liquors of the region.

[7] The *dorobantzi* were a special corps of Rumanian infantry [Nizet].

[8] *Mamaliga* is a porridge made from maize, allegedly the staple diet of Rumanian peasants [Nizet].

[9] In Friedrich Schiller's allegorical ballad *Der Taucher* [The Diver] (1797), a King hurls a golden goblet off a cliff into the sea, challenging his knights and vassals to recover it, and thus claim it for their own. A young page who accepts the challenge is dragged into the depths by a whirlpool. He returns, miraculously, after a magical underwater journey, but the King throws the goblet back into the sea and challenges him again, this time promising a knighthood and his daughter's hand as the reward for its recovery. The boy, fervent with de-

sire to marry the Princess, jumps in for a second time, with the predictable result.

[10] *Selbovitza* is a kind of strong liquor [Nizet].

[11] Unlike Ion Heliade Radulescu, the Rumanian poets Cezar Bolliaco (1813-1891) and Vasile Alecsandri (1821-1890) were still alive at the time when the story is set. Alecsandri similarly played a significant role in the revolutionary upheavals of 1848.

[12] The *hora* is a Rumanian folkdance [Nizet].

[13] This relationship of *frère de lait*, for which English has so better equivalent than "foster-brother," plays a significant role in 19th-century French fiction. It had long been common practice in continental Europe for aristocratic women to "farm out" their children to wet-nurses rather than take on the ignominious burden of breast-feeding. Most European aristocrats of the 18th and 19th centuries thus had "foster-siblings" of much lower social status, with whom they were connected by peculiarly intimate and frequently enduring bonds. The practice was a boon to novelists desirous of forging connections between the social classes that would facilitate their plotting.

[14] A Rumanian *pogone* is slightly less than half a hectare [Nizet].

[15] *Doïne*–the word is plural–are Rumanian folksongs [Nizet].

[16] *Braga* is millet beer [Nizet].

[17] A *zmeu* is a fantastic creature that plays a considerable role in Rumanian superstition [Nizet]. It is a shapeshifter, although it usually appears in human guise–often with a precious stone set in its head–and often flies through the air, sometimes spitting fire. It is a symbolic manifestation of pagan evil, often featuring in folktales as the thief of something vital–which the story's hero must recover–or as a sexual predator.

[18] *Zmeine* is the plural of *zmeu* [Nizet], although Nizet subsequently employs *zmeï* in that capacity.

[19] There is a pun here; *autres moins naïve* [others less naïve] is phonetically identical to *autres moines naïve*; although the literal meaning of the latter phrase is "other naïve monks"

*moines* is also used abusively to mean "bed-warmer." It is difficult to convey, in translation, the sarcastic disdain with which this entire sarcastic passage is saturated.

[20] The Hungarian count Gyula Andrassy (1823-1890) was the first Premier of Hungary; his tenure lasted from 1867-71; he is named here because Tokay dessert wine originated within his domain, and it was therefore assumable that he had the pick of it. He was a close friend (and reputed lover) of Elisabeth, Empress of Austria. This paragraph–as is obvious even in English–is replete with sexual innuendo.

[21] *Romanul* was the title of a newspaper founded in 1857 by Constantin A. Rosetti (1816-1885), a literary man and political leader much influenced by French culture and political ideology, who played a leading role in the revolutionary upheavals of 1848. The paper was closed down in 1864 because Rosetti opposed the first ruler of united Rumania, Prince Alexandru Ioan Cusa, but Cusa was ousted in 1866 and publication was resumed. In the war that forms the background to Nizet's story, both Rosetti and Cusa's replacement, Prince Charles (or Carol), took part in the historic Danube crossing.

[22] The names of the Comanescu children are ironically significant, in a manner typical of transfigured fairy tales (the reader has already been notified of the likelihood of such resonances, and will find more in the next chapter). The two "ugly sisters," Epistimia and Agapia, derive their names from *episteme* and *agape*, the former signifying rationally-derived knowledge and the latter being the name given to the Christian "love-feast," so they are being drawn in archetypally contrasting terms. In French, "Relia" is not so much reminiscent of reliability as of something rebound, like a book, while his full name, Aurelio, means "golden;" the fact that the boy's family nickname–he has another, far more telling, as the next paragraph will reveal–retains a faint echo of *Cendrillon*, the French version of Cinderella, may be coincidental, although he is certainly cast in a Cinderella role relative to his sisters. Alas, the next "ball" to which Relia gets to go will bring him into contact with an

161

extremely uncharming prince, whose invitation to dance is a vicious one. The aftermath of that encounter is certainly not a wedding from his point of view.

[23] These formulas are the equivalents of *au revoir, bon voyage* and a French expression translatable as "stay healthy" [Nizet].

[24] *Rubias* were gold coins minted in the Ottoman Empire [Nizet].

[25] *Galbeni* were gold coins [Nizet].

[26] A *leï* is equivalent to 100 francs [Nizet], or four pounds sterling.

[27] The Yezidees are a Kurdish sect based in Armenia and the Caucasus. Their quasi-Manichean creed–presumably descended from Zoroastrianism, but having incorporated Christian and Islamic elements–sometimes used to be mistaken by ignorant commentators for devil-worship.

[28] A *bani* is equivalent to fifty *centimes* [Nizet], or slightly less than a shilling.

[29] Mihai Viteazul, or Michael the Brave (c.1558-1601) was Prince of Walachia, Transylvania and Moldavia; he was the first to unite the territories comprising modern Rumania, and thus became a significant hero of 19th-century Rumanian nationalism. He joined a Christian alliance against his former masters, the Turks, and fought numerous battles against them; in one of them, he captured the citadel of Giurgiu.

[30] *The Monastery of Argis* (or *Argisch*) is a Rumanian folk-ballad based on a 13th-century legend, in which a company of master masons, headed by the celebrated Manoli (or Manol), undertake to build an unparalleled monastery for Prince Radu the Black on the bank of the Argis river. Radu threatens Manoli that if his masons do not succeed in realizing his dream, he will have him walled up in the monastery's foundations. Unfortunately, the work they do is continually undone by some mysterious agency, and Manoli is told by a disembodied voice that the monastery will never be completed unless the first woman to present herself the following morning is walled up alive in the foundations. It turns out to be his wife, Flora,

so he resolves to trick the Prince with a charade–but Radu sees through the ruse and causes all the masons to fall to their deaths, leaving Flora to die in her makeshift tomb. The song is, of course, a rather ominous choice on Mariora's part.

[31] These are the Rumanian equivalents of *mama* and *papa* [Nizet].

[32] Nicopolis, or Nikopol, a settlement founded by the Emperor Trajan at the beginning of the second century A.D., is nowadays too small to feature on the maps in Atlases, but it occupied a significant strategic position in 1877 by virtue of its situation at the confluence of the Danube and the Iatrus, on what is now the Bulgarian side of the border. It was the site of the first significant victory in the Russo-Turkish war; the Russians took the town on July 16, 1877 and retained it as a base during the siege of Pleven.

[33] *Bashi-bazouks* (*Bachi-bouzouks* in the French spelling) were Turkish irregular troops notorious (according to Webster's Dictionary) for "turbulence and cruelty."

[34] Nizet's *poussah* is a term derived from a sort of toy that simulates the motion of a tumbler; here, as with other terms of abuse used in this and other chapters, I have substituted something that has a similar flavor of contempt to the original rather than attempting to preserve unintended literal meanings.

[35] "My darling" [Nizet].

[36] *Calaretzi* are Rumanian cavalry [Nizet].

[37] "Who goes there?" [Nizet].

[38] "Friends!" [Nizet].

[39] Sardanapalus was the name given by Greek writers to the last of he great Sargonid kings, Asurbanipal (668-626 BC). He secured the Assyrian Empire by means of ruthless oppression, but also presided over a significant flourishing of art and literature, assembling a large library (whose archaeologically-excavated residue is now in the British Museum). Inevitably, he won a reputation in envious Greece–and hence in western legendry–for decadence and debauchery as well as magnificence.

[40] Even in a text that is unusually frank, in its own sly fashion, this surname–which translates as "lovely bush"–is a trifle crude; Relia is presumably as blissfully unaware of the *double entendre* as he is of his intended role in the unfolding orgy. It is unsurprising that his archetypal image of womanhood should reflect the goddess Athene rather than Aphrodite.

[41] Nizet's *fillette au chien* is a *double entendre*; I have given the seemingly-intended meaning, since "little bitch" would normally be rendered *fillette du chien*; both *fillette* and *chien* have other slang applications, widening the potential range of implicit meaning.

[42] An opuscule is, literally, a "little opus"–in this case, a brief essay.

[43] Although *piper* is featured here (at least ostensibly) as the name of a dance–previously advertised as a crude Rumanian version of the cancan–the term is replete with significant meanings in French. Derivatives of the verb *piper* are mostly used with reference to catching birds by means of a sonic decoy, and, by extension, to all manner of beguiling deception and confidence trickery; more crudely–and far more relevantly, in the present context–they include a slang term for fellatio parallel to the Anglo-American "blow[-job]."

[44] I have used the most usual English spelling of "khanjar," although Nizet probably intended to use a calculatedly-Westernized spelling in rendering it *kangiar*; the weapon in question is a short curved dagger originated in the Islamic world.

[45] *Golos* means "Voice;" the word appears in the titles of numerous Russian periodicals.

[46] Codrean is allegedly the hero of a Rumanian ballad [Nizet], but the word simply means "forest" in Rumanian; if it had an acute accident on the e–there is none in Nizet's text–it would mean "forest-dweller," which would be more easily transferable to a particular individual.

[47] "Help! Help!" [Nizet].

[48] A friendly sound familiar to Rumanians [Nizet].

[49] A famous horse of Rumanian legend [Nizet]; *Cal* is Rumanian for horse, so the legendary horse's given name may have been simply Vintesh, but I have been unable to track down any original reference. (Cazacu's version of the text misprints Calul as Caiul.)

[50] "Long live Russia!" [Nizet].

[51] A water-jug [Nizet].

[52] A coin of the smallest denomination, akin to a French *sou* or a English farthing [Nizet].

[53] Literally, "many years"–a formularistic expression of gratitude [Nizet].

[54] "Good day, brother" [Nizet].

[55] A Rumanian proverb [Nizet].

[56] A Rumanian expression signifying Death [Nizet].

[57] An igumen (Nizet has *igoumêne*) or hegumen is the head of a relatively small Orthodox monastery–the equivalent of an abbot in the Roman church; the head of a larger and more important Orthodox monastery is known by the more familiar title of Archimandrite.

[58] These two characters are "rigorously historic," according to Nizet's brief footnote, but I can only identify one of the two families: the Capsas were notable confectioners and restauranteurs from 1856, when Anton and Vasile Capsa founded a confectionery in 1856, until well into the 20th century.

## FICTION

Marcel Allain & Pierre Souvestre. *The Daughter of Fantômas*
Anicet-Bourgeois. *Rocambole*
Guy d'Armen. *Doc Ardan: The City of Gold and Lepers*
Aloysius Bertrand. *Gaspard de la Nuit*
Lucien Dabril. *Rocambole*
Victor Darlay & Henry de Gorsse. *Arsene Lupin vs. Sherlock Holmes 3: The Stage Play*
Alexandre Dumas. *The Return of Lord Ruthven*
Jean-Claude Dunyach. *The Night Orchid: Conan Doyle in Toulouse*
Paul Féval. *The Blackcoats: The Invisible Weapon*
Paul Féval. *The Blackcoats: 'Salem Street*
Paul Féval. *Captain Phantom*
Paul Féval. *Gentlemen of the Night*
Paul Féval. *John Devil*
Paul Féval. *Knightshade*
Paul Féval. *Revenants*
Paul Féval. *Vampire City*
Paul Féval. *The Vampire Countess*
Paul Féval. *The Wandering Jew's Daughter*
Paul Féval, *fils*. *Felifax, The Tiger-Man*
Arnould Galopin. *Doctor Omega*
Victor Hugo, Paul Foucher & Paul Meurice. *The Hunchback of Notre-Dame*
Jean de La Hire. *The Nyctalope vs. Lucifer*
Maurice Leblanc. *Arsene Lupin vs. Sherlock Holmes 1: The Hollow Needle*
Maurice Leblanc. *Arsene Lupin vs. Sherlock Holmes 2: The Blonde Phantom*
Gaston Leroux. *The Phantom of the Opera*
Jean-Marc & Randy Lofficier. *Robonocchio*
Jean-Marc & Randy Lofficier (eds.). *Tales of the Shadowmen 1: The Modern Babylon*

Jean-Marc & Randy Lofficier (eds.). *Tales of the Shadowmen 2: Gentlemen of the Night*
Jean-Marc & Randy Lofficier (eds.). *Tales of the Shadowmen 3: Danse Macabre*
Xavier Mauméjean. *The League of Heroes*
Frank J. Morlock. *Sherlock Holmes: The Grand Horizontals*
Charles Nodier, Antoine Beraud & Jean Toussaint Merle. *Frankenstein*
Charles Nodier. *Lord Ruthven the Vampire*
John William Polidori. *Lord Ruthven the Vampire*
Eugène Scribe. *Lord Ruthven the Vampire*
Brian Stableford. *The New Faust at the Tragicomique*
Brian Stableford. *The Stones of Camelot*
Brian Stableford. *The Wayward Muse*
Brian Stableford (ed.). *News from the Moon*
Villiers de l'Isle-Adam. *The Scaffold and Other Cruel Tales*
Villiers de l'Isle-Adam. *The Vampire Soul and Other Sardonic Tales*
Philippe Ward. *Artahe: The Legacy of Jules de Grandin*


## NON FICTION
Stephen R. Bissette (ed.). *Green Mountain Cinema I: Green Mountain Boys*
Jean-Marc & Randy Lofficier. *Shadowmen: Heroes and Villains of French Pulp Fiction*
Jean-Marc & Randy Lofficier. *Shadowmen 2: Heroes and Villains of French Comics*
Randy Lofficier. *Over Here: An American Expat in the South of France*